PENGUIN CANADA

RUN

Eric Walters is the author of twenty-six acclaimed and bestselling novels for children and young adults. His novels have won numerous awards, including the Silver Birch, Blue Heron, Red Maple, Snow Willow and Ruth Schwartz awards, and have received honours from the Canadian Library Association Book Awards and UNESCO's international award for Literature in Service of Tolerance.

Eric resides in Mississauga with his wife, Anita, and children, Christina, Nicholas and Julia. When not writing or touring across the country speaking to school groups, Eric spends time playing or watching soccer and basketball, or playing the saxophone.

To find out more about Eric and his novels, or to arrange for him to speak at your school, visit his website at **www.interlog.com/~ewalters**.

Also by Eric Walters

Trapped in Ice
The Hydrofoil Mystery
The Bully Boys
Camp X
Royal Ransom
Camp 30
Elixir

Other books by Eric Walters

Death by Exposure
Off Season
Tiger Town
Ricky
Road Trip
Northern Exposures
Long Shot
Tiger in Trouble
Hoop Crazy
Rebound
Full Court Press
Caged Eagles
The Money Pit Mystery
Three-on-Three
Visions
Tiger by the Tail
War of the Eagles
Stranded
Diamonds in the Rough
STARS
Stand Your Ground

RUN

ERIC WALTERS

PENGUIN CANADA

Published by the Penguin Group

Penguin Group (Canada), 90 Eglinton Avenue East, Suite 700, Toronto, Ontario, Canada M4P 2Y3
(a division of Pearson Penguin Canada Inc.)

Penguin Group (USA) Inc., 375 Hudson Street, New York, New York 10014, U.S.A.
Penguin Books Ltd, 80 Strand, London WC2R 0RL, England
Penguin Ireland, 25 St Stephen's Green, Dublin 2, Ireland (a division of Penguin Books Ltd)
Penguin Group (Australia), 250 Camberwell Road, Camberwell, Victoria 3124, Australia
(a division of Pearson Australia Group Pty Ltd)
Penguin Books India Pvt Ltd, 11 Community Centre, Panchsheel Park, New Delhi – 110 017, India
Penguin Group (NZ), cnr Airborne and Rosedale Roads, Albany, Auckland 1310, New Zealand
(a division of Pearson New Zealand Ltd)
Penguin Books (South Africa) (Pty) Ltd, 24 Sturdee Avenue, Rosebank, Johannesburg 2196,
South Africa

Penguin Books Ltd, Registered Offices: 80 Strand, London WC2R 0RL, England

First published 2003

4 5 6 7 8 9 10   (TRS)

Run was written with the generous permission of the Fox family
and the Terry Fox Foundation.

*Publisher's note: This book is a work of fiction. Names, characters, places and incidents either
are the product of the author's imagination or are used fictitiously, and any resemblance
to actual persons living or dead, events, or locales is entirely coincidental.*

Manufactured in Canada.

NATIONAL LIBRARY OF CANADA CATALOGUING IN PUBLICATION

Walters, Eric, 1957–
Run / Eric Walters.

ISBN 0-14-331218-9

1. Fox, Terry, 1958–1981—Juvenile fiction. I. Title.

PS8595.A598R85 2003a   jC813'.54   C2002-902562-4
PZ7

Visit the Penguin Group (Canada) website at **www.penguin.ca**

For Terry

Foreword

For some time, educators, parents and supporters of the Terry Fox Foundation have expressed the need for a Terry Fox book written for the young reader. At the same time, the Foundation has been inundated with requests from writers eager to tell Terry's story. While we have always acknowledged the worthy goal of sharing Terry's story with today's youth, we long ago made the decision not to pursue these projects, abiding by Terry's wish, expressed in the mandate of the Terry Fox Foundation, that his example of courage and hope be used specifically to raise money for cancer research through the annual Terry Fox Run.

Over the years, however, the demand for such a book has grown, and with that in mind, the Foundation recently reconsidered its longstanding position. And so the search began for an author who could tell Terry's story in a way that would reach a younger audience.

We began by approaching all those who had expressed interest in this initiative in the past, and that is how we came to
choose Eric Walters. Eric Walters's passion for writing this
story, together with his philanthropic mindset, were a natural fit
with the mandate and philosophy of the Terry Fox Foundation.

Of tremendous importance to our family was a factual
presentation of the events that relate to the Marathon of Hope;
equally important was an accurate portrayal of Terry's charac-
ter. Further to this, Eric willingly allowed family members to be
part of the process from the early stages of *Run*. For this we are
truly grateful. Eric also introduced us to his editor, Michael
Schellenberg, and to the wonderful and enthusiastic team at
Penguin Books Canada. We were moved by Penguin's sincere
desire to be a part of the project, together with the company's
willingness to offer support for cancer research through the sale
of *Run*.

When Eric suggested a story with elements of both non-
fiction and fiction, it was with some trepidation that we first
considered it. These feelings were short-lived. It was a very
emotional experience for all members of our family to read the
first draft of *Run*. We are immersed in the story of Terry Fox
through our varied involvement in the Terry Fox Foundation.
However, to read words from Terry that he did not actually
speak, but could have spoken, has had a tremendous impact on
all of us. We are also delighted that Doug Alward has found a
prominent place in *Run*. Doug, in his unselfish act of giving up
a year of his life to drive the van during the Marathon of Hope,
truly defined friendship. He played a critical role as the only
member of the Marathon of Hope to accompany Terry from
Day 1, in St. John's, Newfoundland, to Day 143, when Terry

was forced to end his run in Thunder Bay, Ontario, due to a recurrence of cancer. His role will never be measured.

It is of immense comfort to our family to know that Terry's story will be shared with the next generation in a way that would certainly meet with Terry's approval. We are truly thankful to Eric Walters and to everyone at Penguin Canada for bringing this publication to fruition.

Betty, Rolly, Fred, Darrell and Judi Fox
August 2003

Chapter One

THE POLICE CAR SLOWED DOWN and then came to a stop.

"Is this the building?" one of the officers asked me. I was in the back seat of the cruiser, and he had to talk through the metal screen that separated me from them.

"This is it," I answered.

The cops climbed out of the car, slamming the doors shut behind them. They walked to the front and then stood there talking. I could see them, but of course I couldn't hear what they were saying. There weren't any handles on the insides of the back-seat doors so I was trapped in the little cage until they decided to let me out. Even if there had been handles it wouldn't have done me much good because of the cuffs binding my hands behind my back.

Finally one of them—the big cop—came around to the side and opened up the door.

"Get out," he said gruffly as he reached in, grabbed me by the arm and pulled me out of the car. I banged my head against the door frame as he dragged me out.

"Oh, yeah, watch your head," he scoffed, and his partner started to laugh.

"That was pretty careless of him, wasn't it," the first cop—the old one—said.

I was tempted to say something, but thought better of it. Keeping my mouth shut now would be the first intelligent thing I'd done all night. When these two had first caught me I'd smart-mouthed them. All it had got me was these cuffs digging into my wrists.

"Here, let me have him," the older cop said. I was all right with that—the big guy scared me. He grabbed me by the arm and walked me toward the door of the building. The big cop was already inside the first door, standing at the directory panel.

"What's the entry code to get in?" he barked at me.

"Zero-one-nine-eight-five, and then push the star button," I said.

He punched in the numbers and then pulled at the door. A little red light flashed and the door remained closed as he tugged against it. He tried it a second time and the same thing happened. Again he used his big, fat, clumsy cop fingers to try to input the number. The light flashed red and I chuckled.

"Are you sure that's the code?" he demanded.

"I could do it for you if I wasn't wearing these handcuffs," I said. "Couldn't they come off?"

"Soon enough," the cop at my side said. "This is what we have to do to make sure you aren't going to try to run again."

"Where am I going to run to now that—?"

"Are you sure these are the right numbers?" demanded the big cop.

"I'm sure," I said. *Are you sure you know all your numbers?* I thought but didn't say.

Suddenly the door buzzed and a little green light flashed. The big cop grabbed the door and pulled it open. He entered and I followed after him, the older guy still holding me by the arm. We stopped in front of the bank of elevators and he pushed the call button. Almost instantly a door glided open and we entered.

"What floor?" the big cop asked.

"Penthouse."

"Penthouse? How *ritzy*." He pushed the button and the elevator door closed and we started up.

"Nice building," the older cop said.

"Nicer than either of you two could afford," I muttered under my breath.

Suddenly the big cop spun around, grabbed me and slammed me up against the wall of the elevator.

"I've put up with enough from you, you little punk!" he muttered through clenched teeth.

"Slow down, Bob," the older cop said.

"He thinks this is some sort of a joke!"

"Come on, he's not worth it!" He laid a hand against the other guy's arm.

"I just don't like little pukes like this who think they're better than everybody else . . . little pukes who've been wasting our time and keeping us from doing our jobs because they run away from their cushy little penthouse apartments!"

"He's not worth it," the second cop said again. "Let him go . . . let him go."

The elevator pinged and the door started to open. Slowly he eased his grip, and I coughed as I took a deep breath.

"You're lucky this building isn't taller," he said as he released me completely.

The older guy took me by the arm and guided me out of the elevator.

"Which way?" he asked.

"Left . . . it's number five," I sputtered.

The big cop pounded his fist against the door and the sound thundered down the hall of the apartment building. There was no way my mother—or anybody else on the floor—could have missed the knocking. I shuffled my feet nervously. This wasn't going to be pretty. It never was.

"This *is* where you live, isn't it, kid?" the big cop asked.

I started to nod my head when through the door we could hear the sound of the chain being unhooked. The door opened and my mother appeared.

"Sorry to disturb you, ma'am. Is this your—?"

"Winston!" she exclaimed as she stepped out into the hall and wrapped her arms around me. "Are you all right?"

"Sure . . . I'm fine. I was—"

"Your hands!" she exclaimed, cutting me off. She spun me around slightly to look at them. "You're in handcuffs!"

It wasn't like she was telling me anything I didn't know. The cuffs were digging painfully into both wrists.

"We had no choice but to—"

"Had no choice but to place a fourteen-year-old boy in handcuffs?" my mother demanded.

"That's right," the old officer said. "Now, do you want to continue this discussion out here in the hall where *all* your neighbours can hear, or can we step inside your apartment to explain the situation?"

Despite everything, I had to stifle the urge to chuckle. Without knowing my mother, he knew her—she was always worried about what everybody would think. Neighbours, family, people she worked with . . . even total strangers.

My mother retreated back into the apartment and we followed. Just before she closed the door she poked her head out into the hall and looked both ways.

Then, "Could you please take the handcuffs off?" my mother said.

"Certainly, ma'am," the older cop said.

His partner dug into his big belt and pulled out a small metal key. He grabbed me by the arm and spun me around. I felt the cuffs tighten and dig even deeper into my left wrist.

"Quit squirming around," he ordered.

They tightened again, but I tried to stand still and not cry out. I didn't want to give him the satisfaction of knowing how much this was hurting. The cuff dropped off my left hand and I brought my arm around to examine it. There was a deep red mark around the entire wrist.

"There," the big cop said as I felt the cuff come off my other hand.

I brought it forward. It had a matching mark on the wrist. I rubbed my left wrist with my right hand. They both hurt, but that one hurt more.

"Mrs. MacDonald, I'm Constable Esplen," the older cop said, "and this is my partner—"

"I'm not Mrs. MacDonald," my mother said. "I'm *Ms.* Evans."

The big cop turned to me and scowled. "Your name better be MacDonald," he snapped.

"It is! My name really is Winston MacDonald!" I protested.

"Good!"

When they'd first caught me I'd refused to give them my name, and then I'd given them a made-up name. That was all part of what had got them so angry.

"And I'm Constable James," the big cop said.

"Where did you find him?" my mother asked.

"An alley just off Yonge Street."

My mother turned to me. "What were you doing downtown in the middle of the night?"

"Mostly running from them," I replied. "And I would have gotten away if that alley hadn't been blocked."

"Don't take that tone with the officers!" my mother snapped. "Answer my question. Just what were you doing there?"

I didn't say a word. She could make me do a lot of things, but she couldn't make me talk if I didn't want to.

"We know there was some alcohol involved," the big cop said.

"You were drinking?" she demanded angrily.

I was going to say as little as possible. It drove her crazy.

"Maybe if we all could just sit down and talk," the officer asked. "Is your husband home?"

"He might be," my mother said coldly. "Of course, this isn't his home now and he isn't my husband any longer."

"Oh," the older cop said. The look on his face and the tone of his voice in muttering that one word said volumes—things like

That explains everything—it would be different if there were a man in the house.

"I was raised by my mom," the big cop said. "It's not easy being a single parent."

"His father hasn't been living with us for almost two years," my mother continued.

"But I see him all the time," I said, defending my father.

"And when was the last time one of those visits took place?" my mother snapped. "It's been weeks!"

"It hasn't been that long. Besides, he's busy."

"Too busy for his—?"

"How about if we put that away for now," the older officer said, cutting her off. "It's late. We just need to ask a few questions before we can leave . . . okay?"

My mother nodded. "Come this way, please."

She led them down the hall and into the living room. I trailed behind as she motioned for them to take seats. The big cop pulled a pad of paper and a pen from his pocket before he sat down.

"We have to get some information," he began. "We need your full name and date of birth as well as your son's."

My mother answered his questions and he made notes in his book. He looked as clumsy writing as he had trying to punch in the entry code for the building. I was tempted to say something, but I kept my mouth shut.

"How long has your son been on the run?" the big cop asked.

"Nearly two days. I know better than to call the police until he's been missing for at least forty-eight hours."

"It sounds like he's run away before."

She laughed slightly. "Three times over the past few months."

"What's making him run?"

"I wish I knew," she said, her voice barely a whisper.

I knew what was going to come next. Her eyes began to well up and then tears rolled down her cheeks. She quickly turned her head.

"Does your mother beat you up?" the big cop asked, turning to me.

"What?" I asked, not believing what I'd just heard.

"Does she beat you up? Does she hit you?"

"No, of course not!"

"Does she feed you, take care of things, buy you clothes?"

"Well, yeah, but—"

"I don't want to hear no buts," he snapped, cutting me off. "You got life better here than most kids do. Do you feel like a big man making your mother cry like that?"

"No, I—"

"You're just a selfish little snot who figures he can do whatever he wants to do and doesn't care about—"

"Please, that's enough!" my mother said. "He's a good boy . . . he is . . . he really is . . . he was never any trouble," she said, and then she looked like she was fighting back the tears again. "It's just been the last year or so . . ."

The old cop walked over and put a hand on her shoulder.

"I've been doing this job for a long time, ma'am," he said. "And sometimes what's needed is a little time and a little space."

"What do you mean?" she asked.

"Is there someplace your son can go for a day or two? You both could probably benefit from a little time apart."

"We've *been* apart . . . he's been on the run!"

"I mean a safe place. Maybe a family friend, or a grandparent's house."

"There's nobody," she said, shaking her head.

"How about his father's home?" the big cop suggested.

"His father?"

"Does he live in the city?"

"He does . . . but . . . but . . . I can't call his father," she said.

"Does he know what's been going on?"

"I've told him things . . . most things," she admitted.

"Maybe it's time to tell him *everything*. After all, he's still the boy's father, and I bet you'd want to know if the shoe was on the other foot, wouldn't you?"

My mother nodded. "You're right . . . thank you."

The two cops got up from their seats. They shook hands with my mother. Then the big cop came over and stood right in front of me, towering over top of me.

"I don't want to see you again," he said softly. "And I'll take it very *personal*-like if you end up on the streets tonight after we leave. Do you understand?"

I didn't answer.

"Do you understand my meaning?" he asked, no longer speaking softly.

"Sure . . . yeah . . . you want me to stay home."

"Or wherever your mother arranges."

"Sure," I said. That was an easy promise to keep. I was tired and dirty and hungry. I wasn't going anywhere. At least not tonight.

"Good."

"Why don't you give his father a call now," the second cop said.

"I can't call him now. It's the middle of the night."

"You have to let him know what's happening. Everything. And the time to start is right now." He paused. "Okay?"

She shrugged and then nodded ever so slightly.

"In the morning it's too easy to dismiss things. Call him now, wake him up, and let him know that this is important enough to miss some sleep over."

The two of them turned and walked out, leaving me alone with my mother.

Chapter Two

"WHERE DO YOU THINK YOU'RE GOING?" my mother demanded.

"I'm going to the kitchen," I said.

"I'm calling your father."

"You can do that without my help," I snapped. "You know the number."

"Don't you give me attitude!" she shot back.

"I need something to eat," I said. "It's been a while since I ate."

"I'm going to ask your father to take you for a few days," she called out after me.

"Whatever," I tossed back over my shoulder.

"You need to be here when I speak to him."

"I need to eat," I said as I walked out of the room and into the kitchen.

I pulled open the fridge and grabbed the milk pitcher and a hunk of cheese. On the counter I found an apple and a banana.

I'd had nothing but fries and doughnuts and Coke for the past two days. I poured a big glass of milk and drank it down in one big gulp, then refilled the glass.

When I peeked around the corner back into the living room my mother's back was to me, and she had the phone up to her ear. I heard her say something but couldn't make it out. I moved over to the kitchen counter and quietly picked up the extension, covering the mouthpiece with the palm of my hand.

"Don't you know what time it is?" my father said angrily. "It's almost three in the morning!"

"I know perfectly well what time it is," my mother answered.

"Perhaps you know the *time,* but you've obviously lost your sense of *timing.* Whatever this is, it could certainly have waited until—"

"It's about our son."

There was a pause.

"Is Winston all right?" he asked. There was concern in his voice.

"He's fine . . . well, not fine really, but he's here . . . he's safe."

"Then what's wrong?"

There was an even longer pause.

"The police just brought him home, and—"

"The police!" he exclaimed. "Why was he with the police?"

"He was on the run again," my mother said. "Two days. They found him downtown . . . they think he's been drinking. That's why I'm calling. I'm at the end of my rope. I can't take it right now. I was hoping that he could come and spend some time with you."

Again, there was no answer right away. Didn't he want to see me?

"I'm going away on assignment early tomorrow morning. I'll be back in a few days and I can take him out to a movie or—"

"I'm not talking about you taking him to a movie! I want him to come and spend a few days with you. Stay with you."

"Didn't you hear what I said?" he snapped. He sounded annoyed. "I'm going on an assignment. Maybe when I get back I can—"

"You can't be going far if you're only going for a few days," my mother argued.

"I'm not . . . just out to the East Coast, to Nova Scotia . . . two days at the most."

"If you're just going out East for a couple of days then he *could* go with you."

"This isn't a holiday; this is work. You should know as well as anybody what it's like to be on assignment. Or has that cushy television job erased your memory of what it's like on the road for a *real* reporter?"

"I remember perfectly, and that's why I know he can go with you. It's not like you're taking him into a war zone . . . unless somebody invaded the Maritime provinces while I was busy doing my *cushy* television job."

"If there had been an invasion I'm sure you would have read about it in the newspapers," he said. "Who knows, it might even have made it to TV."

My father worked for a newspaper and my mother for a television news show. Newspaper people thought television was nothing but fancy images read by empty talking heads, and the television people thought the newspaper people had to get with the times and that the world was passing them by.

There was a stony silence and neither talked for a few seconds.

"And what if I need to interview a confidential source?" my father asked.

"He's fourteen. You can leave him in the hotel by himself for a couple of hours. What story are you covering, anyway?"

"It's a nothing story . . . human interest angle."

"I didn't think you did human interest stories."

There was no answer from my father.

"I thought that was the sort of *fluff* that television news shows handled. Not the sort of thing a *real* reporter would cover." She sounded amused.

"Unfortunately, there can't always be a war or disaster to report," my father replied.

"So it's settled. He'll come with you," she said.

He didn't answer.

It seemed like my mother was working hard to get rid of me, while my father was working just as hard not to take me. It felt special to be so wanted.

"What about school? Wouldn't it be better if he came with me during the summer? I wouldn't think he could afford to miss any more school if he's been on the run already."

"He can't afford it, but there isn't much choice. Either way, he's not going to school."

"What do you mean?'

"He's been suspended . . . again."

"What do you mean 'again'?"

"He was suspended at the start of the year for two days."

"What for . . . what did he do?"

"He was skipping classes," my mother said.

"And isn't that brilliant!" my father exclaimed. "The boy doesn't go to school, and for punishment they won't *let* him go to school, so he misses more classes!"

"It didn't make much sense to me either, but there's no arguing with school administrators."

"You should have called me. You should have told me."

"Winston didn't want you to know. Despite everything, he still doesn't like to disappoint you. He begged me not to tell you and he promised it wouldn't happen again."

"And?" my father asked.

"Another promise he didn't keep."

"How long was he suspended for this time?" my father asked.

"Two weeks."

"Two weeks! Did he kill somebody?"

"He was caught drinking on school property. And then when they searched his locker they found a screwdriver."

"A screwdriver . . . so what?"

"They said it was a weapon."

"A screwdriver isn't a weapon; it's a tool!"

"That's what they called it."

"That's outrageous! There are dozens of reasons why somebody might have a screwdriver in his locker," my father protested.

"None that your son could come up with."

Of course I wasn't going to use it as a weapon. The reason I had it was that I was planning on using it to break into people's lockers. I just figured that telling them that wasn't going to get me in *less* trouble.

"Why haven't you talked to me about any of this before now?" my father demanded. "Why didn't you tell me he was on the run?"

"I've tried. It's not the sort of thing that you leave on an answering machine."

"You could have just asked me to call," my father said.

"I did leave you messages. At least three."

There was a pause. "I don't always get my messages. My machine has been acting up, and—"

"Do you forget who you're talking to?" my mother asked. "I was there when you didn't return your first wife's calls."

There was an even longer silence. I wondered which of them was going to break it.

"It sounds like there isn't much choice," my father finally said.

"No, there isn't," my mother agreed. "When do you leave?"

"Tomorrow. I catch an eight-fifteen flight, so I'm expecting an airport limo at six-thirty. I'll have the driver swing by and get him just after he picks me up."

"I'll have him packed and ready to go."

"How about if you bring him downstairs and meet us at the door to the building. I'll be tight for time," my father said.

"What else is new?" my mother asked sarcastically.

"This isn't the time for *that* discussion."

"You're right . . . I'm so tired . . . and worried."

"There'll be nothing to worry about for the next few days. He'll do just fine . . . won't you, Winston?"

I froze at the mention of my name.

"I know you're on the extension. One of the things I learned long ago is that you have to slip your hand over the mouthpiece *before* you pick it up to listen in."

I held my breath.

"I'll see you both tomorrow," my father said. "I'm going to try to get at least a little more sleep."

Chapter Three

"CAN I GET ANOTHER DRINK?" my father asked the flight attendant.

"Certainly, sir." She had a big smile on her face. She was blond and perky, the sort of flight attendant they always have on television commercials so you'll want to fly with their airline.

"And make this one a double."

"Yes, sir," she said and hurried down the aisle.

My father turned to me. "That's just one of the many things I like about first class—service with a smile. Shame about this new ban on smoking, though . . . three hours is too long to wait between drags. You want anything? Another Coke, some peanuts, a pillow?"

"I'm fine."

"If you're so fine, how come you haven't put together more than two words since I picked you up this morning?" he asked.

"I guess I don't have anything to say." At least, nothing I

wanted to say to him. What I really wanted was just to be left alone to catch up on my sleep.

"Then it's probably wise to stay quiet. Most of what gets people in trouble is talking when they have nothing to say."

"Here's your drink, sir," the flight attendant said.

He took the drink with one hand and offered her the empty glass with the other.

"Excuse me . . . I was just wondering . . . are you Winston MacDonald?" she asked him.

"Why, yes, I am," he said. He sounded pleased.

"I thought I recognized you from the picture on your news-paper column."

"It's not a very good picture," my father said.

"Do you think you could do me a *big* favour?" she asked.

"Depends on the favour."

"I have today's paper up in the cabin, and I was just wonder-ing if you could autograph it for me."

I could almost see my father's chest puffing up with pride.

"Not a problem," he said. "Not a problem at all."

"I'll be right back." She giggled as she disappeared down the aisle once more, and he leaned slightly out from his seat to watch as she walked away.

"It's funny how often that happens," he said, now looking at me.

Not as much as it used to, I thought, but I didn't say anything. When my father was on the TV news program as well as writing his newspaper column, he was a lot better known. Funny, back then he didn't seem to think TV was such a bad thing.

That was where my parents met. He was a big-time corre-spondent and she was a copy editor . . . really, a junior copy editor. My father had once told me it was a "June and

September" relationship. That was his way of saying that he was almost twenty years older than my mother.

They were married for nearly twelve years. I guess they separated because by that time she was becoming a "July" or "August" and he was still looking for somebody from the earlier part of the calendar. At least that's what you'd have to think judging from the women—or really girls—he dated after he and my mother separated. Those girls all seemed closer to *my* age than his. For sure they were closer to the age of his two sons from his first marriage.

"Remember the time I broke that big government corruption story?" my father asked.

"Which government? Which corruption?" I asked.

He smiled. "You're right, there've been a few. Anyway, you have to remember this one. We were down in Vancouver just after that and we were eating in that little restaurant, that one right by the ocean, and people kept on coming up and—"

"I've never been to Vancouver."

"Sure you have! We were at that little restaurant—you have to remember that restaurant—and the story had just broken across the whole country. Everybody was congratulating me and asking me for my autograph and—"

"That wasn't me."

"Sure it was. I remember we were—"

"It was Dean," I said.

"Dean?"

"You remember him. One of your sons from your *other* marriage."

"Come on now, Winston, I don't think I've done anything to deserve that tone of voice or attitude."

He'd done *lots* of things to deserve that attitude. Lots. And maybe it wasn't Dean, but I knew it wasn't me, which meant my father was wrong. My father didn't like being wrong. And the only thing harder for him than being wrong was admitting he was wrong.

"Think about when that story broke and the year that I was born and you decide if it was me," I said.

He didn't say anything. Maybe he was thinking through the situation . . . or maybe not.

"Here's the paper, Mr. MacDonald!" The flight attendant beamed as she reappeared and thrust the newspaper into his hands.

"Please, call me Mac . . . everybody does. 'Mr. MacDonald' sounds like somebody's father."

He *was* somebody's father. He was *my* father. I was having a hard time trying to figure out what was so wrong with that.

"Sure . . . Mac," she said.

My father looked at the paper as though he were studying it intently. But he wasn't wearing his glasses. They were safely tucked away inside his jacket pocket. I knew that without those glasses he couldn't possibly read what was written there. In fact, he wouldn't know if he was looking at his column or the horoscope page. He hated wearing them, especially since he'd begun using bifocals—he called them "old men's glasses." Then again, he was an old man.

"Not one of my better columns," he said.

"I thought it was *wonderfully* written," she gushed.

"One tries," he said, "but it's a challenge to come up with some-thing every day. Especially when you realize that whatever you write is going to be read by over four hundred thousand people."

"I had no idea it was that many!"

"Closer to a million for my Saturday column," he added. "Now, how would you like me to inscribe this?"

"Um . . . if you wouldn't mind, how about 'To Judy, one of my most faithful readers.'"

"That sounds good."

"Do you need a pen?" she asked.

"Not necessary," he replied, pulling a pen out of the same pocket that was hiding his glasses. "No writer worth his salt would ever travel anywhere without a pen or two in his pocket."

He put the pen to the paper, wrote what she'd asked and then signed it with a flourish, like he'd just done something wonderful.

"Thank you!" she said excitedly as she took the paper back.

"My pleasure," he replied. "So, do you make this flight from Toronto to Halifax very often?"

"Three times a week."

"And are you stationed out of Toronto or Halifax?" he asked.

"Toronto."

"Me too," he said with a laugh. "So, how long is your turn-around time in Halifax?"

"It's different on different flights," she said. "But this time it's a long delay. I work a return flight to Toronto tomorrow afternoon so I stay overnight in Halifax."

"I'm in Halifax tonight too," he said. "Say . . . I was wondering if perhaps you could do *me* a favour, Judy."

"Oh, *my* name isn't Judy, it's Jennifer."

"It is?" he asked, sounding confused. "But you had me sign the column to Judy, or did I hear you wrong?"

Maybe his hearing was going as well as his eyesight.

"I could change it to Jennifer," he offered.

"Oh, no. I wanted it made out to Judy. Judy's my *mother*. She's such a big fan of yours! She's going to be just thrilled to get this!" she said, tapping the paper. "She never ever misses one of your columns, and I remember when I was little she used to watch you on TV all the time . . . that *was* you, right?"

"Yes . . . yes, it was me," he mumbled.

It was obvious that some of the wind had been taken out of his sails. I tried to keep the smile off my face, which was hard considering what I really wanted to do was laugh out loud.

"I was pretty young back then, in middle school, but I used to watch too . . . sometimes . . . if there was nothing else on. Now, you were going to ask me for a favour," she said.

"Yes . . . if it's not too much trouble . . . do you think that you could . . . could bring me another drink?"

"Another? You've hardly touched the one I just—"

She stopped mid-sentence as my father tipped back his glass and drained it, leaving only the ice cubes clinking together.

"And make sure this one is a double too."

I worked harder to smother a smile. I could guess what the favour was going to be. He'd been about to ask her out before he found out it was her *mother* who was the big fan. Well, maybe he could have asked her if her *mother* was willing to go out on a date!

"Certainly," she said as she took his now empty glass. "And does your grandson want another Coke?"

Grandson? Oh, she meant me!

"He's not my—"

"Thanks," I said, cutting him off and handing her my empty glass.

"You're welcome," she said, taking the plastic glass and heading down the aisle.

This was wonderful, simply wonderful! I pulled my earphones up off my neck and back over my ears. I knew I wouldn't be the only one who wouldn't feel like talking now.

Chapter Four

THE ELEVATOR DOOR OPENED. We stepped in and my father pushed the button for the twelfth floor.

"So, were you impressed with that restaurant?" he asked.

"It was okay."

"It's probably the most exclusive restaurant in all of Halifax. I'll bet you would have been more impressed if you'd had more to eat. You should have tried something more expensive."

"I didn't want something more expensive. I wanted a club sandwich and fries."

My father chuckled. "Did you see the expression on that waiter's face when you ordered? He looked like he was going to squirm right out of that fancy tuxedo of his! I think you might have been the first person in the history of that establishment to order a 'club sandwich on white, toasted, with extra mayo.'"

"It's what I wanted."

"Was it at least a good club sandwich?"

"I've had better," I replied.

The elevator came to our floor and we exited. Our room—1220—was right across the hall. My father turned the key and opened the door to the hotel room. He flicked the light, illuminating the suite. It was big and luxurious. No surprise there.

"Remember," he said, "when I'm on assignment everything is covered by my expense account, so you have to live large. Go first class or don't go at all, that's what I always say."

This trip had been classy and expensive all the way. The airport limo, the first-class flight, this hotel suite looking like something out of a movie, the rental car that was waiting for us downstairs, the restaurant—I was impressed. Not that I'd ever say anything, but I was. It wasn't like Mom and I lived in poverty, but this was all top of the line. That was just like my father.

"So, your mother told me about some of the problems you've been having."

I remained silent.

"School can be pretty boring," he said.

"You're not kidding," I agreed enthusiastically.

"When I was in school it just seemed to me like nothing they were trying to teach me had anything to do with the real world," he continued.

"Exactly!"

"And that's why I used to skip classes so often," he said.

"You cut classes?" That was about the last thing I'd expected him to say.

"All the time." He laughed. "But don't go telling your mother that I told you about it. She already thinks I'm responsible for most of the ills of the world and I'd prefer she didn't blame this on me too. So don't rat me out, okay?"

"I won't," I said. What were the chances I was going to tell her about this conversation when I didn't tell her anything about anything else anyway?

My father pulled out a package of cigarettes, put one in his mouth and lit it. He exhaled a puff of bluish smoke that spiralled up into the air. I coughed.

"Filthy habit," he said. "Hope you never take it up."

"I'm too smart for that," I said, taking a less than subtle shot at him.

"Good. You don't have to make all the same mistakes as your old man. See if you can find yourself some new and interesting errors to commit," he said, poking me in the shoulder with his free hand. "You know, the only people who don't make mistakes are those who are too timid to try new things. Stay bold, take chances and be prepared to make bold mistakes. Little people make little mistakes. Big people make big mistakes."

That was certainly strange advice. Did he think I should run away from home longer and get more lengthy school suspensions? How about just suggesting that I try not to make *any* mistakes?

"A writer's got to be prepared to take chances," he said.

"Did you always want to be what you are?" I asked. I didn't want to answer any of his questions, and the best way to avoid them was to change the subject. And the best subject to change it to—one I knew he never ever got tired of talking about—was him and his job.

"So, you want to know if I always wanted to be a reporter," he said.

I nodded.

"Haven't I ever talked to you about this stuff before?" he asked.

"Maybe some of it, but I like hearing about it."

He smiled. What I'd just said actually was sort of the truth. I did like it when he talked about his work and his adventures. It seemed to me that he did have a pretty exciting job and that he was really, really good at it. Sometimes I thought that was the problem—how could me and Mom and our lives compare to the things he did for work?

"I wanted to work for a newspaper as far back as I can remember. Other kids wanted to be firemen or cops or lawyers or teachers or doctors. Me? All I ever wanted was to work for a paper. Do you know what my first job was?"

I shook my head.

"You sure I haven't told you this before?"

Again I shook my head. Although I was pretty sure I'd heard this story, I just couldn't remember it right now.

"I delivered newspapers. That way I could at least feel like I was part of the newspaper family. Then my first job as a reporter was working for my high school paper. I covered sports and wrote articles about what was wrong with the school. Do you have a newspaper at your school?"

"I don't think so."

"Too bad. Maybe there'll be one at your high school next year. If there isn't, maybe you'll want to start one," he suggested. "I was in grade eleven when I became the editor of the school paper. I loved that job! It was probably the only thing that kept me from dropping out of school long before I did!"

"Dropping out long before you did?" I questioned. "What do you mean by that? You didn't drop out of school."

"Well . . . I guess I did sort of drop out."

"*Sort of?* What does that mean?" I asked.

"I never got my high school diploma."

"But you had to . . . you went to university. You took journalism . . . you have a master's degree, right?"

He took a long drag on his cigarette. "I *do* have a master's degree in journalism from Carleton," he said.

"So you *did* go to university."

"Just for one afternoon, to pick up the degree."

"I don't understand."

"I didn't go to school. They gave me an honorary degree for speaking to the graduating class at the convocation."

I was shocked. "So . . . so you didn't *earn* the degree?"

"Of course I earned it!" he protested, sounding offended. "I graduated from the school of hard knocks, the school of real life. I learned more in my job as a reporter than those snot-nosed kids ever learned in journalism school! Schools don't turn out reporters as much as they turn out—"

"Didn't Mom get her degree in journalism from Carleton?" I asked. "And Dean?"

My father opened his mouth to say something and then closed it up again without uttering a word. I would have liked to have had a camera to capture such a rare and magical moment— my father speechless. Now, without a picture, nobody would ever believe it had actually happened.

He stubbed out his cigarette in the ashtray. "Have you given any thought to what career you might want to pursue?" he asked.

"Well," I said with a shrug, "if I keep skipping school maybe I could become a journalist."

He shot me a disapproving look, then smirked and chuckled. "It certainly is a career that's in your blood. It's one that's been successful for your father and your mother and one of your brothers."

"Half-brother," I corrected him. "Different mothers, remember?"

"I know perfectly well that you and Dean have different mothers."

"I was just—"

"I know exactly what you were doing, and I'm not going to take that attitude from you. I'm not your mother!"

"And if you were, would that make it all right?" I asked. Maybe I had been giving my mom an attitude, but it was the same attitude he'd been giving her for as long as I could remember.

"It's never all right, but your mother seems more willing to put up with it!"

Suddenly the phone rang, stopping me from saying what I was going to say—that marriage had given my mother plenty of practice in dealing with bad attitudes.

My father picked up the phone. "Mac here," he barked, and then he listened to a reply I couldn't hear. "Fergy, you old dog, how did you know I was in town?" he asked loudly.

He nodded his head in response to something said at the other end.

"I know you're an investigative reporter, Fergy. I just never thought of you as being a particularly *good* investigative reporter, so I'm surprised you managed to track me down!"

He covered the mouthpiece of the phone and turned to me. "Old friend . . . worked together on the *Telegram*."

I nodded.

"I'd like to join you, Fergy, but I have my kid with me . . . no, not Dean, my youngest, Winston Junior."

There was another reply I couldn't hear.

"No, he's only fourteen so I think he's a little young to have a drink with us."

He pushed the receiver slightly off to the side. "He thought you could come with me to the bar. Wouldn't you agree that you're a little young to be drinking?" he asked me, trying a little too obviously to make a point.

I didn't answer. Screw him.

"Well, I guess I could . . . maybe . . . let me check."

He put the phone down and turned back to me again. "I've been invited to join Fergy and a couple of other guys for a drink. Would it be okay if I popped out for a while?"

"Sure, whatever."

"Because if you don't want me to, then I'll stay here and—"

"I'm not your mother *or* your wife, so go if you want!"

He smiled and brought the phone back up to his ear. "How about we meet in ten minutes at Dooleys?" He listened to the reply. "No, there's no need to pick me up, I can walk from here. Why do you think I booked into this hotel? If you're not there when I get there, I'll start without you."

He replaced the phone in the cradle.

"Another reason to work for a paper is that you end up with friends in every city. You can always find somebody to chum with." He looked at his watch. "I don't think I'll be too long. Watch some TV, order from room service if you want. Remember, it's all paid for by the paper. If I get hung up longer than I plan, tuck yourself into bed and go to sleep. It's going to be an early morning tomorrow."

"I'll take care of myself," I said. "I'm good at that."

He gave me a look, like he was going to say something, but he changed his mind. He grabbed his jacket from the back of the chair then stopped at the door and checked to make sure he had his wallet, keys, lighter and cigarettes.

"Oh, while I'm thinking about it, you should call your mother. I told her I'd call when we arrived to let her know how everything was going," he said. "I guess I should have called earlier. Give her a call."

I nodded.

"See you later," he said, and the door clunked shut noisily behind him.

I walked over and picked up the phone. There were instructions written on a card beside it to explain how to get the hotel operator or the outside operator, and how to make long distance calls and reverse the charges and . . . I put the phone back down. I wasn't going to call. Let her worry.

I walked back to the bed and glanced at the door. Maybe I should go out for a while too—there had to be a video arcade somewhere around here, didn't there? Popping a few quarters and playing a few games would be a good way to kill the evening. But I really didn't have any idea where to go . . . did they even have arcades out here, or was it just in big cities like Toronto?

Or instead of just heading out for a while, I thought, maybe I should go out for a *long* time. Wouldn't that shock him, if he got back and I wasn't here. I could just picture him getting all worried and calling my mother and . . . then again, maybe that wasn't such a smart idea. I was a long way from home and I was tired. I needed at least one good night's sleep.

I sat up, startled by a noise, and for an instant I didn't have a clue where I was. The only light in the room was the glow of the television, which was showing a test pattern and buzzing. The station had gone off the air for the night. What time was it?

I climbed off the bed. I was still wearing my clothes. I walked across to the dresser and picked up the clock. It was after one in the morning and my father still wasn't back! He'd left just after eight o'clock. Gone for a little while . . . sure. I wasn't surprised, but it didn't make me feel better to be right.

I clicked off the television and the room was dark. The only light was the Halifax night coming in through partially drawn curtains. I was edging across the floor when my attention was caught by sounds coming from the hall. Was somebody having a fight or. . . ? It was singing. I recognized the voice.

I ripped back the covers on my bed, jumped in and pulled them back over top of me. As I turned over, the singing became louder and then stopped altogether. I heard the sound of a key fumbling for the lock and the door opened. Light from the hall flooded into the room. I closed my eyes tighter and tried to at least pretend I was asleep.

Chapter Five

I SLUMPED DOWN IN THE SEAT and stared out the window. If nothing else, the car certainly had big, comfy seats. If only I'd kept the earphones from the airplane I could have blocked out my father humming along to the music blaring on the radio. How did he always manage to find a station playing Frank Sinatra? Even worse, why couldn't he just let the man sing by himself? Frank Sinatra was bad. Frank Sinatra *and* my father singing was almost more than I could handle.

He'd already been through his third coffee of the trip and more cigarettes than I bothered counting. He said the combination of the two was the only thing that kept him awake, which I guessed was good, since he was driving. He obviously hadn't had much sleep the night before. I hadn't had much either after he'd arrived home. I'd tried to sleep but couldn't get my head to shut off.

"Could we turn that down a little?" I asked.

"What's wrong, don't you like Sinatra?"

"You have to be joking. I doubt there's a teenager in the whole country, in the whole *world,* who likes Sinatra."

"That's probably because they haven't given him a chance." He reached over and turned the volume up instead of down. "They call him the Chairman of the Board, Old Blue Eyes. The man has *style.*"

"Old-fashioned style maybe," I countered.

"He defined style for a whole generation."

"Not this generation."

"So what singers do you like?" he asked.

"I don't like singers. I like groups. Like Yes, King Crimson, Led Zeppelin and Pink Floyd."

"Pink Floyd . . . I think I've heard of him."

"It's not a *him,* it's the name of a group," I said with disdain.

That shut him up for a minute. Now, if only Mr. Sinatra, the Chairman of the Board, would do the same. I had no problem with him doing it "his way" as long as he did it more quietly, or someplace where I wasn't.

"Now that I've given it a chance, can you turn it down?" I asked.

"Sure," my father said as he reached over and adjusted the volume. "You ever been to Nova Scotia before?" he asked.

"Never. You?"

He laughed. "I've been everywhere before, but Nova Scotia is where I'm from."

"It is?" I asked.

"I'm surprised you didn't know that."

Clearly, there was a whole lot I didn't know about him. "I remember you telling me something about you being born out East but I didn't know where . . . or at least I don't remember."

"I was raised in Halifax from the time I was ten." My father laughed. "Where did you think I was from?"

"I never really thought about it. You said the East but it just always seemed to me like you were born and raised in Toronto . . . maybe the *east* end of Toronto."

"I'll take that as a compliment," he said. "Although many people wouldn't."

I didn't mean it as anything, but he could take it any way he wanted.

"I was brought up no more than a five-minute walk from where we stayed last night."

"You said you were raised in Halifax. Does that mean you weren't born there?" I asked.

"Nope. I was born in a small town. Jerkwater, Nova Scotia."

"Jerkwater!" I exclaimed. "You're joking, right?"

He chuckled. "I am. That's what we used to call it when we were kids. It's actually called Millwater."

"I've never heard of it."

"No surprise there. Nobody's ever heard of it. It's just a little nothing dot on the map."

"How many people live there?"

"A better question is how many people *survive* there. It's tiny. One store, a gas station and a smattering of houses hanging on for no apparent reason. The only good thing about the town was that we finally left it."

We drove along in silence—well, silence except for the music on the radio. Mr. Sinatra had been replaced by some cheesy-sounding trumpet blaring out of the speakers, and my father had turned up the volume again.

"It would be hard for you to understand what it's like to live in a place like Millwater because Toronto is the only place you've ever lived. It's a pretty exciting city."

"I like it."

"It's not like London or L.A. or New York—actually, no place in the world is like New York—but it's still a big city, and people can get in a lot of trouble in a big city."

I was smart enough to know where this was going.

"So tell me, what do you do when you're on the run?" he asked.

"Nothing."

"You're saying the last time you were on the run you did nothing for two days?"

"That's right."

"You must have done something. What did you do?"

"Hung around with friends . . . ate . . . saw a couple of movies . . . slept at friends' places."

"Hanging around usually leads to trouble."

"I didn't get into any trouble."

"Then why did the police pick you up?" he asked.

"It was the middle of the night and they saw a kid. That was the only thing I was doing wrong."

My father leaned over and popped in the cigarette lighter. He then fumbled around in his pocket and pulled out his package of cigarettes, took one out and put it in his mouth. The lighter popped out and he put the end to his cigarette, puffing until it caught. He replaced the lighter and then exhaled a puff of smoke.

I pushed the button and the window on my door glided down

slightly. I would have preferred the car to be filled with Sinatra than with smoke.

"I got in my fair share of trouble when I was a kid," my father said.

I knew this trick. He'd tell me something and then hope I'd tell him something in return.

"Did I ever tell you about the times I was a kid around fourteen and tangled with the police?"

"I don't think so."

"There were more than a few, but let me tell you about one that happened when I was about your age. Maybe a little older. Maybe a little younger. Anyway, my friends and I were walking down this alley in Halifax when we found a whole pile of old car tires that were being thrown out, and we started to play with them . . . you know, rolling them around."

"Gee, that sounds like fun," I said sarcastically.

He ignored my jab. "So now that you've seen a little of Halifax you have to realize that the whole city is on a hill, and this alley was right at the top of a *very* high hill. We started wondering what would happen if we aimed those tires down that hill. So we pulled them all out—there had to be twelve, fifteen tires. And were just getting ready to let them go when we saw a car coming up the hill . . . a police car." He paused. "Do you know what we did then?"

"Ran like crazy?"

"We did that . . . after we pushed the tires down the hill toward the police car."

"You didn't."

"We did. We took aim and then let those tires go shooting down that hill! You should have seen them! Some just fell down, but most of them gathered speed and went faster and faster and faster and BAM! A couple of them bashed right into the front of the car. One jumped over the bumper and then hit the hood and rolled right up the windshield and over the car!"

"Wow, that must have been amazing!"

"It was! And *then* we ran like crazy!"

"Did the police catch you?"

"They tried, believe me, they tried! They called in other cars and there were police zipping all over the neighbourhood! We hopped over fences and got back to Danny O'Mallory's place and spent the rest of the day hiding under his front porch where we could see the street but nobody on the street could see us. Do you know what those cops would have done if they'd caught us?" he asked.

"I can imagine."

"They would have beaten the tar out of us. That's what cops did in the old days. Very different from today. Police have to be downright gentle today."

I could still feel that cop's hands shoving me up against the wall of the elevator. Some things apparently hadn't changed as much as he thought.

"So . . . what sort of things have you done that have got you into trouble?"

"Nothing," I said, shaking my head. "Nothing at all."

I had to fight to keep the smirk off my face. That wasn't even a good try. Either he was losing it or I was getting smarter. Maybe both.

"Can I ask you a question?" he asked.

Could I stop you if I wanted? I was thinking, but I didn't say anything. He took my silence as a yes.

"Why do you run away?" he asked.

"I don't know," I said. That was maybe the first completely honest and truthful thing I'd said to him this whole trip. I had no idea why I did it. I just did.

We continued to drive along in an uncomfortable silence. Maybe he'd give up and leave me alone now.

"You haven't even asked me about the story I'm covering," my father said, again turning the conversation around. "Aren't you curious?"

"I figured you'd tell me sooner or later."

"There isn't much later left. We're almost there. So, do you want to hear about it?"

"Sure . . . I guess. Can we turn down the music?"

My father hit the volume button again. I could still hear it, but the engine noise and the rush of air through my window almost drowned it out.

"We're going to be meeting with a young man named Fox, Terry Fox. He's running across Canada to raise money for cancer research."

"Hasn't that been done before?" I asked.

"The running across Canada part or the raising money for cancer part?" my father asked.

"Both."

"I don't know, but there's a slight twist at work here," he said. "This young man . . . he's twenty-one . . . he's a survivor of a bout with cancer. A bout that cost him one of his legs."

"One of his legs?" I questioned. "Do you mean he's *hopping* across Canada?"

"Not really hopping. He has an artificial leg. You ever known anybody with an artificial leg?"

I shook my head. I knew that my father was going to tell me some story about somebody he used to work with when he was a reporter at some newspaper who had a false leg or—

"I used to work with this guy who had one leg," he began.

I almost laughed out loud but stopped it halfway up my throat.

"He lost it during the Korean War—stepped on a land mine. Well, anyway, he always used to complain how much that stump hurt, how it got sore and infected sometimes, and how much work it was to do things like climb stairs or even go for a long walk. I remember once he and I went out after work one day and we went to this bar and . . ." He paused. "Maybe I should save that story until you're a little older."

As far as I was concerned he could save that story as long as he wanted. "Yeah, so what about this story you're covering?"

"Oh, yeah, so this Fox kid is trying to run across the country. Every day he's running an average of twenty-six miles—that's forty-two kilometres. It's the equivalent of a marathon every single day! Quite an accomplishment, don't you think?"

I shrugged. "Depends on how long he's been doing it."

"He started in early April in St. John's, Newfoundland, so he's already put in over seven hundred miles in the last five weeks."

"He's travelled a long way," I admitted.

"Of course that's only a fraction of the distance he's planning on running, less than 15 percent of a trip across the country."

"Do you think he can do it?" I asked.

"I don't think *anybody* can do it, even on two legs. That's why it's important to interview him now . . . before he quits."

Chapter Six

"SO, WHERE ARE WE MEETING THIS GUY?" I asked.

"We're going to have lunch with him and his friend . . . I can't remember his name . . . Doug something. This is basically a two-man operation. The one kid runs and this other guy drives the van and organizes things."

"I hope whatever restaurant we stop at knows how to make a decent club sandwich," I commented.

"Actually, we're not eating at a restaurant. We're meeting them on the road when they stop for lunch."

"And what are we going to eat?"

"We're brown-bagging it. Lunch is in the back," he said, gesturing over his shoulder. A fairly large cardboard box sat in the middle of the back seat. "And if I'm not mistaken, that's them now."

He pulled the car over to the shoulder. Dust billowed up behind us as he slowed it down and brought it to a stop right

behind an almond-coloured van parked off to the side of the
road. On the side in large letters it said "Marathon of Hope,
Cross Canada Run in Aid of Cancer Research." Shouldn't it have
said "*Trying* to Run Cross Canada Run"?

My father pulled down the visor of the car and took out a pad
and pen. He never, ever went very far without them.

"How about if you get the lunch," he suggested.

He climbed out his door and I was startled by the sound of a
car whizzing past on the road. I grabbed the lunch, pulled it over
the seat and got out on my side.

I turned around to see two guys sitting at a picnic table set off
the road and under a tree. My father walked toward them. I
hurried to catch up.

"Hi!" my father called out.

"Hello," one of the men said back. "Are you Winston
MacDonald?"

"Actually, we're both Winston MacDonald," my father
replied. "Father and son."

Both of the men stood up. It was obvious which one was
Terry Fox when the artificial leg became visible. He had a head
of curly brownish hair and he was wearing a T-shirt with
"Marathon of Hope" printed on it. He looked young. Both of
them looked young.

"I'm Terry. Pleased to meet you," he said as they shook hands.
"And this is my friend, Doug Alward."

"Good to meet you," Doug said, and he shook hands with
my father as well. He was wearing a pair of old jeans and a
shirt like Terry's.

"Pleased to meet you, too," Terry said, and he stuck out his
hand to me.

"Um . . . me too . . . um, Mr. Fox," I muttered, shaking his hand.

"Terry, it's just Terry," he said. "Have a seat."

My father took a seat opposite Terry Fox as the other guy, Doug, shook my hand as well. I took a seat on the bench beside Terry.

My father pulled out his pad and flipped it open. "I hope you don't mind if I take notes. I always try to make sure I have my facts and quotes right."

"Sounds good to us," Terry said. "Not all reporters do that."

"The taking notes, or the getting it right part?" my father asked, chuckling.

"Both," Terry answered with a grin.

"Must be dealing with TV reporters. So, how long are you taking for this break?" my father asked. "How long have we got for the interview?"

Terry looked at Doug, who looked at his watch. "We have about twenty-five more minutes before we should be on the road again. Is that enough time?"

"It should be," my father said. "I have some background already. Let me just run it by you to make sure all the facts are correct."

"Sure," Terry said.

"Your name is Terrance Stanley Fox. You were born in Winnipeg, Manitoba, and raised in British Columbia. Parents are Betty and Rolland. Two brothers and one sister."

"So far so good."

"My notes say you were diagnosed with cancer back in March of 1977."

"A form of bone cancer called osteogenic sarcoma," Terry explained.

"And a few days after making the diagnosis they took the leg off."

"Five days later," Terry said.

"Your right leg," my father continued.

"I'm pretty sure that's the one," Terry said with a smile as he reached down and knocked on the artificial limb.

"So when did you think up this whole idea of walking across Canada?" my father asked.

"I'm not *walking* across Canada, I'm *running*," Terry said. I could hear the annoyance in his voice and he sat up stiffer. "Anybody could walk across the country. I'm running."

What was the big deal? Could he really be running on one leg anyway?

My father nodded. "Yes, of course. Running, and raising money for cancer research."

"I think the running part started the night before they took off my leg. I read an article in a magazine that my old high school basketball coach, Terri Fleming, brought me. He had read the article and thought I should read it too. It was about an amputee runner, a guy who ran in the New York City Marathon."

"That's how you got the idea about being able to run, but when did you get the idea about running across the country?" my father persisted.

"That night," he said. "I know it sounds strange, but I dreamed about it that night while I was lying there in the hospital bed, waiting for them to amputate my leg."

A shiver went up my spine. What would that have been like? Lying in bed, trying to sleep, knowing that when I woke up they'd be wheeling me into an operating room and taking off my—

"I had the idea, but I didn't tell anybody about it right then," Terry continued. "I had to convince myself it was possible before I talked to anybody else about it."

"And the fundraising part?" my father asked.

"That came almost right away too. I saw a lot when I was being treated. I read a lot, and I found out how little money was being spent on research to try to cure cancer."

"Being a cancer victim, you'd certainly be more aware of those things."

"I don't think of myself as a victim," Terry said. "I'm a survivor. A cancer survivor. I got up and walked away from it. Now I'm doing something for those who didn't get a chance to walk away. You have to understand that I'm one of the lucky ones . . . the people who survived cancer. I remember those who weren't so lucky. I've been there in the cancer ward with other people . . . this is my way of trying to make the hurt stop so that other people don't have to suffer or die."

"And when did you start to do something about it?" my father asked.

"That wasn't until a lot later. Like I said, first I had to convince myself that it was possible."

"How did you do that?"

"I started back into playing sports."

"No surprise there," Doug said softly.

Terry smiled. "Wheelchair basketball. Another friend, his name is Rick Hansen, he got me interested in playing. We were the national wheelchair basketball champions three times running. I did miles and miles and miles in that chair during those practices and games, getting myself strong. Sometimes I'd push myself harder than maybe I should have."

"As in he'd do it until his hands started to bleed," Doug said.

"Did you use the wheelchair to get around before you started running?"

"No," Terry said. "I never used a wheelchair except for basketball. I got around at first on crutches, and then with a cane to help, and finally I just started walking and then running with the artificial leg. I started to train. That first day I ran one lap of the track by my house—I did a quarter of a mile."

"And that went well?" my father asked.

"No," Terry said, shaking his head. "It went awful. I couldn't believe how much it took out of me to run that one lap. But I went back the next day and did the same thing. At the end of the first week I added another lap, and then another the next week and the week after that and the week after that. I trained for about fourteen months. Every day except Christmas."

"His mother asked him to take the day off," Doug explained.

"I ran over three thousand miles," Terry continued. "It was than that I knew I could do this."

"And when you did finally tell people about your plans, they must have thought you were nuts," my father said.

"My mother said I was crazy," Terry said, and everybody laughed. "But I told her I was going to run anyway, and she said she'd help any way she could."

"And what was your father's reaction?"

"He just wanted to know when I was going to go."

"They didn't try to talk you out of it?"

"Well, maybe a little bit at first, but they knew I was serious so they just decided they'd get behind me on this."

"That's awfully supportive. And Doug, what was your first reaction when Terry told you about his plans?"

"I just thought, 'If Terry says he's going to do it, then he's going to do it.'"

"And when he asked you to come along?"

"I said, 'Sure, when do we go?'"

"So you didn't need any persuasion," my father said.

"None, although I really had to wonder whether he'd picked the right guy for the job!"

"There isn't anybody better," Terry said, and though Doug ducked his head I could see he was hiding a grin.

"And were you like his parents, or did you have questions?"

"Oh, I had questions," Doug said. "Lots of questions. But no doubts. Terry told me what he was going to do, and I knew he was going to do it, end of story," he said with a shrug of his shoulders.

"You didn't have *any* doubts?"

A slight smile came to his face. "You don't know Terry."

My father laughed. "It sounds like your family and friends really believed in you from the start. It's nice to have people back you up that way," he said. "I was wondering, is it painful to run on that leg?"

"It's not really a problem."

"Really?" my father persisted.

"It can be a little sore sometimes, but nothing I can't handle."

"I see. And what is your artificial leg made of?"

Terry pulled his leg up and put it on the bench right beside me. "Fibreglass, metal, a little bit of leather. It's pretty sophisticated."

"And it has lots of parts that can go wrong," Doug added. "It really takes a pounding out there and it needs to be adjusted and tinkered with all the time to make the spring work right."

"But it's working pretty good today," Terry said.

Doug looked at his watch again. "We have to get going in a couple of minutes."

"It sounds like you're running on a real schedule," my father said.

"We try," Terry told him, "although all the credit for that belongs to Doug. I just do the easy part, the running. He takes care of everything else."

"Sounds like a good arrangement. You two been friends for long?"

"Practically forever," Terry said.

"Must be good friends to spend every day together. How many days has it been?" my father asked.

"This is day forty," Doug said.

"I dipped my foot into the Atlantic on April 12," Terry said.

"In Newfoundland?"

"St. John's."

"The weather in Newfoundland in April can be pretty bad," my father pointed out.

"Bad doesn't even come close to describing it," Doug said. "And I was just driving the van."

"We had some rough days," Terry added. "Snow. Sleet. Rain. Cold. You name it and I ran through it."

"That must have been tough."

"It wasn't easy," Terry said. "But what we found was that even when the weather was cold, the people were always warm and friendly."

"Nice people," Doug said. "It's like everybody in the whole province of Newfoundland is friendly."

"I'll never forget the way we were treated in Corner Brook," Terry added.

"They gave you a good reception?" my father prompted.

"They were great . . . and generous. They made it all worthwhile."

"I have two more questions," my father said. "First, why are you doing this?"

Terry looked confused. "To raise money for cancer research."

"I understand that you want to raise money, but aren't there easier ways than running across the country?"

"Maybe easier, but this is the way I want to do it," Terry said. "By running like this I let people know that cancer can be beaten . . . that life can go on . . . that you define people by their *ability* and not their *disability*." He shrugged. "And your last question?"

"You've probably already answered it, but I'll ask anyway. Do you think you can do it? Do you think you can actually run across the whole country?"

Terry smiled. "You're right . . . I have already answered that one."

Both men stood up once again, and I staggered to my feet as well.

"Thank you for taking the time to interview us," Terry said as he reached out and shook hands with my father first and then with me.

"Thank you for giving me the time," my father replied.

Terry stepped over the bench and then swung his artificial leg over as well.

"Wait a second, I do have one more question," my father said.

Terry turned back around.

"When you're out there running, what do you think about?"

"Mostly I just try to think about the next part of the run. I take it one day at a time, one mile at a time, one corner at a time. I'm reaching out for each signpost and each corner. All you can do is take another step and keep on going."

"But what do you *think* about?"

Terry didn't answer right away. "I guess I think about a lot of things. Sometimes I think about what it's going to be like running into Port Renfrew."

"Is that your hometown in B.C.?" my father asked.

"No, we're from Poco . . . Port Coquitlam," Doug explained. "But Port Renfrew, on Vancouver Island, is the farthest point west, so that's where the run ends."

"That's where I'll put my foot into the Pacific Ocean," Terry added.

"Speaking of which," Doug said, "the ocean isn't coming to us, so we'd better get going."

"Right. I'll see you in a mile," Terry said to Doug.

He walked over to the side of the van, touched it with one hand and then started to run up the road.

It was the strangest run. I don't know what I'd expected, but this wasn't it. He certainly wasn't walking—it was sort of skip- ping or hopping or bouncing along the road. It was . . . it was—

"It's not the most graceful movement," Doug said, reading my thoughts. "But there's something almost hypnotic about it."

"What happens now?" my father asked.

"I clean up, get in the van and drive one mile. Terry catches up to me and I give him a cup of water. I drive another mile, and when he catches me the second time he has some more water, some oranges or a snack and rests a minute. Then he runs the next two miles. We keep doing that until we reach our goal for the day."

"And that goal is how many miles?" my father asked.

"We try to do about twelve miles in the morning and add another fourteen in the afternoon. Some days it's only fifteen altogether, sometimes more than double that, depending on the road we have to cover, or arrangements we've made for spending the night. On average Terry covers twenty-six miles a day, which is forty-two kilometres. Then we mark our spot on the road, go and spend the night in the back of the van, or sometimes someone will donate a motel room, which is great. We start up again the next day where we left off," he said. "Thanks a lot for the interview. I think we've gotten to understand that stories like this really help to raise awareness of what Terry's doing, and that raises money for cancer research, and that's what this is all about. Now I'd better get going or Terry will beat me to the mile spot."

"Thank you. I'll write a good article."

Doug gathered up the plates and garbage from the table and headed for the van.

"We'll just stay here and eat our lunch before we're off," my father said to me.

I'd forgotten all about eating! My father opened the lid of the box and pulled out two paper bags. I opened up the one he handed to me. It held a big, delicious-looking club sandwich— on white, toasted. It looked like it had extra mayo!

I looked up at him and smiled.

"I had a hunch that might be what you'd like for lunch," he said.

"Thanks," I said as I pulled it from the container and took a big bite. It tasted good, very good. Much better than the one I'd had the night before.

"So is that it?" I asked.

"I don't understand," my father said. "You want more than one sandwich?"

"No, no . . . I mean, is that the whole interview? They send you all this way for a twenty-minute conversation?"

"There's a little more we have to do still."

"What?"

"We have one more place to stop," he said.

"Where?"

"First we eat . . . then we drive."

Chapter Seven

WE STAYED ABOUT ANOTHER HALF HOUR at the picnic table finishing our lunch. My father mainly picked at his and had a couple more cigarettes. I couldn't believe how many cigarettes he smoked every day.

My thoughts turned to the two men we'd just met. They seemed so normal and nice. Don't ask me exactly what I'd been expecting, but somehow I guess I'd thought that somebody who was running across the country would be different. Maybe full of himself and cocky, or just downright strange. Like, what normal person really thinks he can run across the country? Especially run across the country on one leg? To even think that you could do that you had to be . . . maybe a little bit crazy . . . although he didn't *seem* crazy.

"Ready?" my father asked.

"All set."

I'd been finished for a while. I actually could have gone for a second club sandwich because the first one was so good. That was nice of him to get that sandwich for me. It was the sort of thing he used to do all the time when I was growing up. He was always doing things to make me happy—even when my mother didn't want him to. She didn't want him to "spoil" me. I *liked* being spoiled!

Besides, I knew that it wasn't just him doing nice things for me. I tried to do things to make *him* happy, too. But that was in the past. Way in the past.

My father was different from other fathers I knew. He always seemed to be full of surprises. You never knew what to expect out of him, but it was almost always something different, or fun, or unusual, or at least not boring. My father was never boring. Even when he came in hours after he was expected—maybe especially then—he was never boring. Maybe boring would have been better. I think my mother would have liked a little more boring and a little less in the way of surprises.

We bundled up the last few pieces of garbage, tossed them into a garbage can sitting just over from the table and climbed back into the car. He turned the ignition and both the engine and the radio started up, playing *another* Sinatra song! My father turned it up and started to sing along as he pulled back onto the highway. I was beginning to think that this guy wasn't the Chairman of the Board, he was the Chairman of the *Bored*.

"You still haven't told me where we're going," I said, using my question as an excuse to turn the radio way down.

"A little town just down the way from here."

"To do what?"

"To watch."

"Watch Terry run?"

"That's only part of it. We'll watch him run. And we'll watch Doug driving that van. We'll watch people watching them. And then I'll probably do some more interviews."

"You're going to interview Terry and Doug again?"

"Nope. Other people."

"What other people?" I asked.

"People in the town. I want to know what their reaction is to what Terry's doing. If I'm not mistaken, I think we can capture something. Something that I don't completely understand, but something that people are going to want to read about, and—"

"There they are!" I yelled.

Up ahead, almost at the top of a long hill, I could see the almond-coloured van crawling along the side of the road. In front of that was the lone figure of Terry running . . . jogging along . . . whatever it was exactly he was doing.

My father slowed down as we got closer. He really didn't have much choice. A number of cars up ahead of us had done the same. It was then that I noticed that vehicles coming in the opposite direction were also slowing down as they passed. Some people rolled down their windows and waved. Others honked—not an angry, get-out-of-my-way sort of honking, just a gentle *tap, tap, tap* of the horn. A car up ahead pulled off to the side of the road in front of the van. The driver jumped out and ran back to the driver's side.

"What is he doing?" I asked.

"Watch . . . reporters learn to watch and watch to learn."

The man reached out and handed something to Doug.

"What did he give him?" I asked.

"If I'm not mistaken, I think he handed him some money."

"Really?"

"Really. You see?" my father said. "Something *is* happening."

We came up alongside the van. My father beeped his horn and I caught sight of Doug—he gave a wave as we passed. We slowed down even more as we reached Terry. He looked over and smiled and his arm shot up to give us a little wave as well. I turned around as we drove past and continued to watch. It hardly looked like he could make it to the top of the hill, let alone across the country.

"When you said we were seeing something happening," I said to my father, "does that mean you think he can make it?"

"Make it?"

"Yeah, run across the country."

"Before we sat down with him I thought there was no way in the world he had a chance of doing it."

"And now you do?" I asked.

"There's something in that kid's eyes. You probably couldn't see it because you were sitting beside him, but I saw it."

"So you think he *can* do it?"

"No, not really, but I think there's a chance . . . not a big one . . . heck, let's be honest, not even a small one, but I think there is a tiny chance . . . maybe."

"Is that what you're going to write?" I asked.

"I don't know what I'm going to write yet. I won't know until I sit down at my typewriter and start pounding the keys. Then the story sort of takes on a life of its own." He stopped and looked over at me. "That sounds sort of strange, doesn't it?"

"Not really. I think I know what you mean."

"You do?"

I nodded.

"Are you still writing?" he asked.

His question surprised me so much that I didn't have time to decide what I *should* say and instead just answered truthfully. "Not any more."

"You were quite the little writer," my father said. "Great imagination, lots of details. I loved your stories."

I knew that. I used to love showing them to him. That was one of those things I used to do to make him happy. He would tell people that he was raising another little reporter.

"Why did you stop writing?"

"I don't know. I just didn't have anything I wanted to write about any more."

"Who knows," my father said, "that could change. Lots of things could change. Well, here we are . . . our destination."

"Here we are?" I asked. "I don't see any *here* here."

"Read the road sign up ahead."

"It says 'Welcome to Millwater' . . . Millwater!"

"One and only. Welcome to the town of my birth."

Just past the sign announcing the town limits my father slowed down and then pulled the car into the parking lot of a store. We kicked up a cloud of dust as we rolled over the gravel.

"Do you know what this is?" he asked.

"A store."

"The general store that your grandfather owned. I was born in the back bedroom of the house attached to it."

"You were born here?"

"Right here. Come on, we'll get ourselves a cold drink."

We climbed out of the car and walked onto the wooden verandah that stretched along the front of the store. My father stopped and turned around.

"Here it is," he said, gesturing grandly. "This is the town of Millwater. Pretty impressive, eh?"

Impressive wasn't the word I would have chosen. Besides the store there was a small gas station just down the way—two pumps. There were houses, well set back from the highway on both sides—maybe twenty or thirty altogether. Farther away, but I guess still part of the town, were a couple of barns and matching silos stretching up to the sky.

"It's pretty much the same as it always was," my father said. "A couple of houses have new siding . . . I can see they've put an extension on the old McPherson place . . . and . . . and that's about it."

"Really?"

"Really. Nothing much changes in a place like this."

"Even the people?" I asked.

"Especially the people. There are people who've been in this town for five generations. I've been gone over forty years and I bet I still know most of the people here, or their relatives."

I wondered if that meant we were going to talk over "old times" with a bunch of people I didn't know and had no interest in ever getting to know.

"Are we going to stop in and visit anybody?" I asked, dreading the answer but needing to know.

"Of course, knowing them and having anything in common with them are two different things. Besides, it's important to stay low-key."

"What do you mean?"

"We're here to observe. Good reporters just sit off to the side and watch. Why don't you grab one of those chairs over there while I go in and get us a couple of pops. A Coke for you, I assume?" he said.

"Nothing else but."

The store's door had a bell that gave a *ping* as my father walked in and rang out again as he closed the door after himself. I sat down on one of the big wooden chairs, shaded from the sun by the roof of the verandah, with a good view of the highway. We'd be able to see Terry as he ran past.

My father soon reappeared with the drinks. "Here you go," he said, handing me my Coke.

"Thanks." I took a big gulp from the bottle. "So, did you know the guy running the store?"

"I think I went to school with him."

"You did?"

"Can't be sure without asking, but his name tag said 'Tim' and he looked familiar . . . about the right age. Got me thinking," he said as he took a slug from his bottle.

"Thinking about what?"

"Thinking that maybe if my family hadn't moved when I was little that might have been me in there behind the counter."

"Come on, be serious."

"I am being serious. My grandfather ran the store, and so did my father up until the time we moved. Who knows?" he said with a shrug. "Who knows."

My father took another sip from his pop and sat there silently, sort of just staring off into the distance like he was trying to see something far away.

"It's a shame your grandfather died before you got to know him. You two would have liked each other."

"What was he like?" I asked.

"He had a real playful side to him. He'd come home from a hard day's work—sometimes twelve hours—and he'd grab a bite to eat and come on out on the street and join in with me and my friends with whatever game we were playing. Didn't matter if it was road hockey or baseball or real hockey down on the pond. He'd just come and join us."

He took another sip and began staring off again. Then he let out a big, deep sigh.

"I guess I never did that for you, did I?" he asked. "Always too busy . . . on the road on assignment or doing something on deadline. There was always a deadline or something else I should be doing."

He was right, there had always seemed to be something that he had to do, something that took him away from me and Mom, something more important. Maybe this was the time for me to say something to—

"Look, here they come!"

Chapter Eight

"THERE . . . FINISHED," my father said. He pushed back his chair, got up from the desk and stretched.

"That didn't take too long," I commented.

"You're talking to a pro, somebody who's *never* missed a deadline in his entire professional life. And believe me, I don't know another reporter who can say that without lying. I'm very proud of that fact. I make a commitment and I keep it."

Obviously he wasn't talking about commitments to his family.

"Besides, while some articles take a long time to write, others practically write themselves."

"And this one?" I asked.

"Maybe you can be the judge."

"You'll let me see it?"

"Why not?" he asked with a shrug. "Tomorrow morning there'll be over four hundred thousand people reading it. Besides, I'd like to know what *you* think about it."

"Wait . . . you want *my* opinion?"

"You're smart, and you were there today. Read it while I refresh my drink."

I clicked off the TV and got up off the bed. This motel certainly wasn't like the luxurious hotel we'd stayed in when we were in Halifax, but it was comfortable.

My father walked over to the dresser and poured himself another drink.

MILLWATER, NOVA SCOTIA—The Trans-Canada Highway gently curves and climbs through the lush countryside. It passes by forests and fields and a scattering of farms and small towns. One of those towns—not much different from the 10 towns before and the 10 that come after—is Millwater.

A sign just on the outskirts signals a reduction in speed. This is more a courtesy than a necessity. It's not like there's much danger of there ever being enough traffic to pose a risk. There are one or two stores, a gas station, a few dozen houses and, well set back from the road, a school.

"Welcome to Millwater—Population 200" is what the sign says. It's an old sign. That same sign was there the last time I passed through 10 years ago. And it was there 43 years before that—the day my family moved away. It said 200 the day before we moved, and it said 200 the day after we moved. It doesn't really announce the population as much as a belief that there should be 200 people here. There aren't. There haven't been 200 people living here for a long time. Maybe never.

Millwater is the sort of place where every conversation starts with a comment about the weather. That says a lot about the realities of living in the country, where everybody's life is a farming life and the weather isn't just an inconvenience but a matter of grave importance. It's not like in the city, where the weather just means taking an umbrella or putting on a sweater. Instead, it defines what can be done and should be done that day. Do you plant, or mow, or fertilize, or harvest? Do you move the herd, or repair fences, or work in the barn? It could also mean the difference between the farm failing or thriving, between money for a new tractor and new shoes for the kids or being able to make the mortgage payments to keep on farming.

My father wasn't a farmer. He ran the general store. I sit on the wooden porch of that store and watch. Beat-up old pick-up trucks and cars pull in, and their occupants amble up. "Do you think it'll rain today?" I've heard that question half a dozen times in the hour I've sat here. Any time it's aimed at me I answer the same way—"Looks like it could."

I spent the first ten years of my life in Millwater. It's a place where not much happens. Not that that's necessarily bad. It just is. Sure, occasionally somebody gets married or buried or born, or a new tractor is purchased. I remember sitting on this front porch as a child and watching the traffic pass by. And I remember thinking that everybody who passed by was involved in something important—going someplace else. It seemed like all around us important events were unfolding. Everywhere except Millwater.

That changed today.

From the east, the Trans-Canada slopes gently down to meet the town. I caught my first glimpse as he crested the hill. A lone figure, moving along the side of the road. He's running, but the gait is different. There's a strange rhythm to his steps. Not step after step after step after step. It's more a long stride, followed by a skip, and then a short step. And the longer you watch, the more this rhythm gets inside your head. And you have no choice. You have to watch.

Cars pass by him in both directions. Some pay no notice, don't appear even to see him. Others slow down, people hanging out of windows, staring, gawking. Some honk their horns and wave. He waves back each and every time—with a little jerky motion he raises his hand and acknowledges them. I wonder how many times he's done that. Others pull right off to the side of the road and get out of their cars and watch, and clap and cheer him on.

As he gets closer you can see the reason for the strange pattern in his gait. While his left leg is strong and muscular, in the place of his right is an artificial limb made of metal and fibreglass. Step after step. Striding forward with his powerful left leg, a small skip, and then a step on his prosthesis.

He moves closer and you can make out his features. He's young—he'll turn 22 later this year. His head is topped with a mop of curly, unruly hair. His face is tanned and handsome. He looks like the boy next door, or a friend of your son's, or maybe the boy your daughter brings home. Not that any boy will ever be good enough for her—but he looks like he might be as close as anybody could be.

If you look at him—and you have to look very closely—you can see a slight twinge on his face when that artificial leg hits the ground. I know it must hurt. I also know he doesn't want people to see that in his face.

Moving in tandem, just behind to protect him from traffic, is a van. As he enters the outskirts of the town the van pulls out and drives off, coming to a stop in the centre of town, in front of the store, right in front of me. The driver's door opens and a man, as young as the runner, emerges. He walks to the back of the van and half leans, half sits against its rear bumper. He's watching his friend, waiting for him to arrive.

Slowly the runner comes. Never faster or slower. That same awkward, entrancing gait, until a few steps before the van he slows down to a walk. The second man greets him, offering a cup of water, a pat on the back and a plate of cut-up oranges—my kids called them "orange smiles." Together they walk to the van, open the sliding door and sit down, their legs hanging out the side.

Just a few at a time, a crowd starts to gather around them. That's something I never thought I'd see—a crowd in Millwater. Hesitantly, almost reluctantly, the runner stands up and starts to talk. His name is Terrance Stanley Fox, but he introduces himself simply as Terry. He tells them that at age 18, while attending first year in Kinesiology at Simon Fraser University, he was diagnosed with cancer, and five days later his leg was amputated. He tells them how that night, while awaiting the surgery to remove his leg, he had a dream to run across Canada to help raise money for cancer research. When he was receiving treatment, chemotherapy, he thought about those all around him suffering and how he wanted to try to do something to help them, some of them just kids. And now, three years later, he's fulfilling this dream. He calls it the Marathon of Hope. Those words are written across the side of the van.

He started his run in St. John's, Newfoundland, on April 12. He dipped his artificial leg into the Atlantic Ocean and began running. That first day he ran 26 miles— the equivalent of a marathon. And the next day he ran 26 miles. And the next, and the next. And here he sits. Forty days, close to a thousand miles, and halfway across his second province. Imagine that—every day for the past 40 days he has run an average of 26 miles, on one leg. It's almost impossible to believe that could be real. But it is.

I listen to the young man. His story isn't polished and professional. He's speaking from the heart, not from a speech he has written down and memorized. It's obvious that he isn't a politician or a public speaker. Sometimes his speech is halting. Sometimes I wonder if he's close to tears. Always he is friendly, genuine and considerate. As I said, he isn't a politician.

Having given his speech, he thanks people for taking the time to listen to his story and asks them to help support the Marathon of Hope—to contribute a few dollars, or perhaps more than a few dollars, to help fight cancer. People come forward and press money into his hands and the hands of his friend, Doug Alward.

He starts to run. Stride, skip, step. Stride, skip, step. The crowd begins to clap and cheer as he runs past the remaining buildings that make up Millwater. More than a few people begin to cry. Not just the women. An old farmer who looks so tough that he wouldn't blink if you hit him in the head with a shovel wipes away a tear from his eye. There's a story there. Maybe it's about his wife or a son or daughter who battled cancer. Maybe won the battle. Maybe lost it. I could ask him, I guess, but I can't. I'm too busy wiping a tear from my own eye.

Nothing ever happens in Millwater. Except today. Today a little piece of history was made. Today a man named Terry Fox passed through town. He's a hero. Terry would tell you different. He'd tell you he's no hero. I'm telling you he is.

I felt shaken . . . my breath taken away. I looked up from the page.

"So what did you think?" my father asked.

I sniffed hard. I couldn't believe it . . . I was fighting back tears. What the hell was wrong with me? "It was . . . it was . . . good."

"Only good?" He laughed.

"Really good."

"And what did you think about the last couple of lines?" my father asked.

"About him being a hero?"

He nodded. "After reading the article, do you think he's a hero?"

"Sure. Of course . . . yes."

My father smiled, a smug sort of smile, and took another sip from his drink. "I'm glad I could make you think that."

"That's what *you* think too, isn't it?" I asked.

"That's what I wrote."

He hadn't really answered my question. "But is that what you think?" I persisted.

"What's important is what people think when they read my story."

I was confused. "But . . . but . . . you *do* think he's a hero, don't you?"

"I think he's attempting something heroic. But it really doesn't matter what I think or don't think. Some people say never let the truth get in the way of a good story. I never agreed with that. The truth is the truth."

He took another sip.

"If you don't think he's a hero, what do you think he is?" I asked.

My father shrugged again. "I didn't say that I *didn't* think he's a hero. Maybe he is, but who knows? Maybe he's a con man, or somebody into self-promotion or a fraud."

"A fraud?"

"For all we know he only runs a few miles on each side of the towns and sits in the back of the van the rest of the way. Or maybe he's keeping all the money they collect for himself."

"Do you really think he does that?"

"I doubt it," he said, shaking his head. "In my business you get to know people. I'd bet that this kid is legitimate. Genuine. Honest. What do you think?"

I struggled to find the words. Before my father mentioned it I hadn't even thought about him not being honest.

"Well?" my father asked.

I shook my head. "I think he's really running . . . that he's doing this to raise money for cancer research . . . I think."

"I'm sure you're right, but it would sure make one heck of a story if he was crooked. The only thing the public likes better than building up a hero is tearing one down. Tragedy sells more papers than triumph."

I didn't know what to say to that. I almost felt stunned—did people really like to read about people failing?

"So you do think that he is doing the running, right?" I asked.

"I think he probably is, but anyone can be fooled. Look, kid, I'm not saying he isn't a hero. Only time will tell. Have you met many heroes in your time?"

"I got the autographs of some of the Leafs once," I said.

"I'm not talking about some joker who plays hockey. I'm talking about a hero, a real hero. Somebody who undertook a brave deed, maybe risked his life—that's what the dictionary would probably define it as," he said. "So that excludes hockey players, rock stars and actors."

I shrugged. "I guess nobody I can think of then."

"I've been around a whole lot longer than you and I haven't come across too many. There were a couple of guys when I was covering wars, a doctor working in the jungles of Africa I interviewed once. You don't come across them every day." He paused. "But maybe, just maybe, this Fox kid is one of them. And if that's the case, you should remember that you've met him." He paused again. "In the end, there's only one thing I know for certain right now."

"What's that?" I asked.

"I know I need another drink."

Chapter Nine

"THANKS A LOT." My father's voice was exuberant as he spoke on the phone. "You're about the tenth person that's already called today to tell me how well the story is running. Yeah, the piece will attract a lot of attention. . . . No, he's very friendly, so I'm sure he won't mind other reporters showing up, even TV people. He's had some local press along the way but nothing on a national scale before."

My father nodded his head and laughed at a comment. "Sure, I'll stop in and see you the next time I'm in town," he said. "Maybe we can have a drink in that little bar just over from the paper. What's the name of that place? . . . Yeah, that's the one! They have the best wings in town and . . . What do you mean it's closed down?"

He listened. "Either way, I'm sure we can find someplace to get together. Thanks for the call." He put the phone down again and turned to me, grinning. "It looks like that little story has made some big waves. That was a friend in Montreal. His paper's sending him down to do an interview and he wanted to know if—"

My father's sentence was cut short by the phone ringing again. It had been like that all morning. We'd picked up the early edition of the paper at a coffee shop near our motel and sampled the local bacon and eggs before heading back to our room. There was nothing else to do today but head back to Halifax for our four-thirty flight to Toronto.

"Hello, Mac here!" he said into the phone. "Good to hear from you!" He turned to me. "It's my editor," he mouthed.

"Did you expect anything less than a great article?" he said with a laugh. "Yeah, I guess you've been passing on this number because I've been getting calls here from . . . You're kidding."

He remained silent and nodded his head. "Well, I guess that *is* a pretty good response. So when I drop into the office tomorrow to pick up my messages I can return some of those calls. Hopefully you'll have something for me to work on and . . . What do you mean?"

My father stood up and walked back and forth, the cord trailing behind him, holding the phone to his ear. I could tell by the expression on his face that whatever was being said to him certainly wasn't making him happy. Had somebody said something bad about his writing?

"That doesn't make any sense at all," he said. "Yes, yes, I know the response has been good, but I've already done the story!" my father thundered.

He began to pace faster and his face became angrier as he continued to listen.

"Look, there's no way I'm going to stay here and—"

He stopped mid-sentence and began listening again. In the silence I could just make out his editor's voice on the other end—not the words, but the tone. He sounded as angry as my father did.

"Yeah, I know you're the editor and the editor is supposed to assign the reporters, but—"

He was cut off once more. Again I could hear the voice on the other end.

"Have you at least got an angle I'm supposed to work for the follow-up story?" my father demanded.

He listened to the answer.

"Great, just great. I'll remember this one," he muttered as he hung up the phone without saying goodbye.

"What's wrong?" I asked, although I had a pretty good idea what had just happened.

"I did such a great job that my editor wants me to stay on the story," he said.

"You have to stay here?"

"Not here. I have to follow Terry and his friend for another day or so and file more reports."

"Am I staying with you?" I asked.

"You were supposed to be with me for a few days anyway. Don't suppose it matters much whether it's here or back in Toronto. Is that okay with you?"

"Whatever. Here's as good as there, I guess."

"How long does your school suspension run for?"

"Tomorrow's Thursday, right?" I asked.

"All day."

"I'm suspended for the rest of this week and the first two days of next week."

"So staying here with me isn't a problem. We'll be back long before that. Get your things packed," he said.

"Packed . . . but you said I was going with you."

"You are, to the next place. My editor told me he's taken the liberty of booking us into the same motel that Terry and Doug are staying at tonight. Apparently he's even made arrangements for us to go out with them and travel in the van tomorrow."

Now *that* sounded like a lot of fun, sitting in the back of a van travelling down the road at a couple of miles per hour.

"Oh, and while I'm thinking about it, we'd better let your mother know we're staying a while longer. You can give her a call while I go and get another pack of cigarettes."

"Sure, I can do that," I said. Although just because I *could* do it didn't mean I *would* do it. I didn't have anything more I wanted to say to her now than I had when I didn't call in Halifax.

MAY 24, 1980

"Come on, Winston, time to get up," my father said as he gently shook my shoulder.

"Get up?" I said groggily. "It's not even light yet." Waking up before dawn in yet another fleabag motel was nothing like the glamorous image I'd always had of a reporter's life.

"It won't be light for a while. It's just after four-thirty. We have to hurry or we'll be late."

"How can we be late for anything at four-thirty in the morning?"

"The van leaves at five. If we're not there they'll leave without us," my father explained.

"Why so early?"

"I imagine they need to leave early to get in the miles they need every day. It isn't like he runs very fast."

I threw off the covers. Getting ready wouldn't take long. I hadn't even bothered to unpack the night before after arriving at the motel so I'd slept in my clothes—a pair of jeans that hadn't seen the inside of a washer in too long and a long-sleeved Pink Floyd T-shirt.

I stood up and staggered into the bathroom. The reflection staring back at me almost made me do a double take. I looked tired, dead tired, and my hair was sticking up in two dozen different directions. My mom always said I got my wild, curly brown hair from my dad, but it was hard to guess that now, when he had barely enough left to cover the top of his head. I wouldn't have time to wash up, but I could throw some water on it and try to comb out some of the wildness.

"There's an all-night diner next door!" my father hollered at me from the other room.

"Do we have time to eat?"

"Not breakfast, but doughnuts."

I chuckled. Doughnuts were my usual breakfast—and lunch and dinner—when I was on the run. Apparently my father and I still did have a couple of things in common.

"Why don't you pick up a dozen or so!" I yelled back. "Lots of chocolate dip! And how about a coffee . . . a *big* coffee . . . double-double!"

"A man after my own heart!" my father called out. "I'll bring my bags with me. You bring yours and I'll meet you at the front door of the motel in five minutes."

I heard the door open, then close.

I splashed water on my face and then some more on my head, trying to soak down my hair. With both hands I flattened it out, trying to somehow make it look less awful. I should have unpacked my comb, but it was buried deep inside my suitcase. If I could have found it I could have found my toothbrush as well, which was, let's face it, even more important. Bad hair was one thing, but I really hated that taste in my mouth when I woke up. I was probably the only person in the world who tried to practise proper dental hygiene when he was on the run.

None of this was going to do much good. I got out of the bathroom and grabbed my bag. Quickly I left the room and hurried down the hall.

"Good night's sleep?" the clerk asked as I passed by the front desk.

I was a little surprised to see anybody else up already. "Not too bad," I said. "I just wish I could have found my toothbrush and some toothpaste."

"Allow me," he said. He reached under the counter and pulled out a small plastic package. "Here, take one of the motel's complimentary kits."

I stopped in my tracks as he handed it to me.

"Brush, toothpaste and a small comb," he said.

"Thanks, thanks a lot."

I opened the door to leave.

"Hope you enjoyed your stay . . . come again!"

"Yeah," I said doubtfully as the door swung shut behind me. I couldn't see that ever happening. This motel was not only in the middle of nothing, it was rundown in the middle of nothing. I knew that Terry and Doug were grateful to get motel rooms donated, but you'd think they could have done a bit better than this! If I were running across the country, I'd want to sleep somewhere a lot nicer than this place.

I took a few steps to the side and sat down on a bench. It was still damp—just like everything else. Damp and dark and misty and chilly.

I put my bag down and tore open the kit with my teeth. The toothbrush was in two pieces and I put them together. Next I opened the tiny tube of paste and squeezed out a bit. I put it in my mouth—minty tasting—and started to brush. Not perfect, but a lot better than doing without.

"Good morning."

I turned around. It was Terry. He was dressed in track pants and a sweatshirt.

"Boy, would your mother be proud of you," he commented, chuckling. "Mine is always reminding me to do things like that."

"I . . . um . . . wanted to get rid of the taste in my mouth," I mumbled through the lather.

"I hate that too. Sometimes you get a seriously bad case of morning mouth, especially if you've been sleeping on your back."

I spat the foam out into the bushes and then deposited the toothbrush back in its bag and stuffed it into the outside flap of my suitcase.

"It's a bit chilly this morning," I said, trying to make conversation because I was uncomfortable with the silence.

"A bit, but it's one of my favourite times to run. Once I'm out there with the moon casting the only shadows, there are no cars, no people—just the shadows of trees and the farms."

I couldn't help but picture that scene in my mind. It did sound sort of nice.

"Do you like to run?" Terry asked.

"I used to do a little cross-country," I said.

"What a coincidence, I'm doing a little cross-country myself," he said with a laugh, and I couldn't help laughing along with him.

"Where's your father?"

"He's coming. He just went to get us some breakfast . . . well, really some doughnuts."

"Doesn't that sort of cancel out the benefits of having already brushed your teeth?" he asked. "So much for your mother being proud of you."

"Good morning!" my father called out as he came up from behind Terry. He was carrying a box of doughnuts and a tray with four steaming cups of coffee.

"Good morning, Mr. MacDonald, I just—"

"None of this 'Mr.' stuff, it's just Mac," my father said, cutting him off.

"Sure, Mac. I just wanted to thank you for the article you wrote."

"Oh, I'm glad you liked it—hope it helps you guys out."

"Yeah, my mother said she got a lot of calls from people about it. She said there's been an increase in the donations. And yesterday we got more requests for interviews—newspaper *and* TV—than any day since we started."

"Just doing my job. Where's Doug?" my father asked.

"He's just making a last-minute call. There are always so many details to take care of."

"I got enough doughnuts for everybody and four coffees. I don't know how you two take them so I just left them black and brought along extra sugars and creams."

"Thanks. Works great for me. But Doug doesn't drink coffee. I'm always telling him a little caffeine might be good to keep him awake. It gets pretty boring driving along a mile at a time." He paused. "And speaking of Doug . . . here he comes."

The van rolled up and came to a stop right in front of us. Doug jumped out almost before it had come to a full stop and hurried around the front to join us.

"Morning everybody. Sorry for the delay. I had to firm something up. There's going to be a television crew from one of the national news shows coming up to film this afternoon."

"That's great!" Terry said.

"Now, we better get going. We're already behind schedule," Doug said.

"We are?" my father asked.

"Yes, it's almost five minutes after five already," Doug pointed out. "Everybody in."

Terry moved over to the side door of the van with that distinctive gait of his. I'd almost forgotten about his leg, with him standing there in track pants. He grabbed on to the side of the van's door and pulled himself up and into the vehicle.

"Why don't you come up front with me," Doug suggested to me. "Terry usually grabs some shut-eye while we drive to the starting spot."

Doug slammed the side door closed and then circled around the front of the van and climbed into the driver's seat.

My father held the passenger door open for me. I climbed in and was instantly struck by the smell—it was awful! It was a combination of sweat, rotting food and some sort of terrible chemical odour I couldn't identify that practically turned my stomach.

My father climbed in the back. "Quite the smell in here," he said.

"I guess we really should clean up a little more often," Doug admitted. "But really, after a while you hardly notice it."

I didn't think if I spent a year in that van I'd ever get to that point.

I looked back over my shoulder. Terry was in the back corner in a small bunk. He'd pulled a blue sleeping bag up around him and his eyes were already closed. I slumped back in the seat and did the same while my father leaned forward to talk to Doug.

"Do we have far to drive?" he asked.

"Twenty-six miles."

"I meant to the starting point. Is it far from here?"

"Only a couple of miles down the road. We always try to sleep as close as we can so we don't waste much time in the van."

We travelled along the lonely highway. The darkness was occasionally broken by the bright lights of a big rig coming down the highway toward us. Except for those trucks there was no other sign of life.

"How do you know the place where Terry stopped running?" my father asked.

"I always have a general idea, and then we look for the marker that shows the exact spot," Doug said. "Matter of fact, we're coming up to it right now."

Doug slowed the van down and pulled it onto the shoulder. "The marker should be right up ahead."

"What does it look like?" my father asked.

"It's a white plastic garbage bag, held down by some rocks and—there it is!" Doug slowed the van even more and then brought it to a stop.

"Are we here?" Terry asked from the back of the van.

"We're here."

Doug climbed out of the driver's door and I got out on the other side.

My father opened the big side door and he and Terry climbed out. Terry put his foot down right on top of the garbage bag. Then he bent down and touched his toes, stretched his leg, twisted and turned at the waist. "So much for warming up. I'll see you all in a mile."

"See you in a mile."

Terry started running, and we stood there watching as he headed out into the darkness and mist. I watched until he got smaller and smaller and then finally disappeared into the black.

Doug bent down and picked up the plastic bag, shaking it free of the rocks and gravel that had pinned it to the ground.

"Do you ever have problems finding the marker?" my father asked.

"Sometimes it's hard. Once it was impossible."

"Impossible?"

"There was a strong wind that night and it must have blown away. We searched and searched but we couldn't find it."

"So what did you do then?"

"We drove back about three miles to a spot we *knew* we'd passed, a spot Terry had run by that day. Terry wanted to make sure that nobody could ever say he didn't run the whole way," Doug explained. "Did you notice how he put his foot down right on the plastic bag?"

I nodded.

"Every inch of the way, from one ocean to the next. Now we'd better get going so we can mark the first mile."

Chapter Ten

My father walked up the highway ahead of the van, puffing away on his cigarette.

"I hope he understands," Doug said.

Terry had been in the van taking one of his breaks when my father had lit up a cigarette. Doug had asked him to smoke outside instead.

I was happy to get him out of the van. He'd been a pain all morning, short-tempered and grouchy. When he did talk, it was to ask me another question about school or home or something else I didn't want to talk about. I knew that he didn't want to be there covering the story—heck, did he think I wanted to be riding in a smelly van?—but that didn't give him the right to be difficult with me.

"It's just that it's hard enough with all the fumes from the cars without the cigarette smoke in here too," Terry added.

"I hate it when he smokes around me," I agreed.

"I take it you don't smoke," Terry said.

"Never. Not even one puff. It causes cancer."

"Yeah, I think I heard that somewhere," Terry said.

"Um . . . yeah . . . I guess you'd know about all that stuff."

Terry and Doug started laughing.

"I've got a phone call to make," Doug said. "I'll be back in a couple of minutes."

Doug left the van and walked toward the gas station.

"So, you live in Toronto," Terry said.

"Yeah. How did you know?"

"Your father writes for a Toronto paper, so I figured you'd probably live there."

"I do live in Toronto, but I live with my mother. My parents are separated."

"I didn't know. How long ago?"

"A long time . . . more than two years."

"But you've stayed close to your father."

"He's on assignment a lot. He travels all over the place."

"Does he take you with him like this very often?"

"Not often," I answered. *Never before* was actually the truth, but I didn't want to say that. Maybe we weren't that close any more, but somehow I still wanted people to think we were . . . maybe because that's what I wanted to believe myself.

"It's nice that you get to spend time with him like this. I always enjoyed doing things with my dad, even little things."

"Yeah, it's okay," I agreed, although so far this morning it hadn't been.

"So what do you do for fun in Toronto?" Terry asked.

"I guess the same as anybody. You know, watch TV, hang around with friends, go to the arcade and play video games. I love video games."

"What games do you like?"

"Pac-Man, Frogger, some of the car-racing games."

"How about Donkey Kong?"

"I like that one too. Actually I like them all. If I had enough money I'd spend all my time at the arcade. There's this really great place on Yonge Street just north of Dundas. Do you play video games?" I asked.

"I never really got into them. My little brother Darrell likes them. I see people play and I've played a game or two, that Donkey Kong game, but I never really had the time for stuff like that. And since I started training for the run I haven't had time for anything, not even playing sports."

"You play sports?" That took me a bit by surprise.

"Of course I play sports," he said, sounding offended. "Any reason I shouldn't?"

"No, not really," I said, although obviously he'd thrown me for a loop. Then I remembered. "That's right, you said something about wheelchair basketball."

"I played on the Cable Cars, three-time national champions. Ever see a wheelchair basketball game?"

"Never."

"You should. It's physical, tough. It makes the game kind of interesting when nobody can dunk and everybody is about the same height. Do you play any sports?"

"I used to. I ran some cross-country, like I said. And I was into soccer and basketball . . . but I don't play so much any more. Just in gym class. That's about it."

"By the way, what happens to school when you're away like this?"

"Nothing really."

"Do they give you extra work to do to make up for what you're missing?" he asked.

"No." I hoped he'd drop the subject. I had no intention of telling him about getting suspended. It wasn't something I was proud of. Even now, it didn't seem like something that could ever happen to me. I used to be a good student . . . well, I guess before.

Terry looked as though he was studying his artificial leg. He was running his hands up and down the side and flexing it back and forth.

"Is something wrong?" I asked.

"I think the spring is a little bit off. It's not snapping back as well as it should. It makes it harder to run. Ever seen an artificial leg before? It's actually an interesting thing. Here, I'll show you."

Without warning Terry reached down and started to undo some straps. Before I even knew what he was doing he was holding his leg and handing it to me! I turned my head just a bit—the thought of looking at the stump where his real leg used to be made me feel a bit sick.

"Here, take it."

I drew back.

"There's nothing to be afraid of," Terry said.

"I'm not afraid."

"It's not like it's going to bite you . . . it has toes, not teeth." He smiled and held the leg out again. Tentatively I reached out and he handed it to me. Gingerly, carefully, I took it from him. I was holding his leg . . . shoe and sock and everything. I was amazed at how light it was.

I turned it around slowly, looking at it from every angle. It looked so strong, powerful, like something the bionic man would have . . . except for the sock. The sock was dirty and worn and I thought it even smelled. I looked at Terry's other foot. That sock was much whiter and cleaner.

"I think you need to change one of your socks," I said.

"You're right. I need to . . . but I'm not going to."

I gave him a questioning look.

"That's the sock that was on my artificial leg when I dipped it in the Atlantic in St. John's, and it's going to be the sock that will be on my foot when I dip that leg into the Pacific."

"You're not going to change it?"

"Nope. I don't even wash it. It stays right there. Do you think that's strange?"

I shrugged. "I once wore the same T-shirt for twenty straight days without washing it."

Terry laughed.

"I thought it would weigh more," I said.

"You mean your unwashed shirt or my leg?" he asked and smiled again.

"The leg."

"It's metal and fibreglass, especially constructed to be light but to take a pounding. It's a lot lighter than the artificial legs they used to have. It wasn't that many years ago that an amputee couldn't have even attempted what I'm doing because the artificial legs were downright primitive. I think people didn't even consider that somebody could lose a leg and still want to be athletic, want to play sports and compete."

"Here," I said, handing him back his leg. He began strapping it back into place.

"Do you have an extra if this one isn't working?" I asked, grateful that he was wearing the leg again instead of me holding it.

"A couple of spares. When I was training for the run I once had one of my legs snap in two . . . fell flat on my face . . . hurt like hell."

"What did you do then?"

"Picked myself up, grabbed the pieces, hopped over to the side of the road and started to hitchhike home."

"You must have got some strange looks from the people in cars driving by," I suggested.

"A few, but not many drove by. I got picked up pretty quick."

"At least you had an excuse to cut your training short that day."

He shook his head. "Got home, clamped the two pieces back together and finished my run."

"You're joking, right?"

He shook his head, and I realized, just from the little I already knew about him, that was what I should have expected him to do.

Doug reappeared at the door of the van. "You ready to go?"

"Is it time?"

Doug nodded his head.

"Then I'm ready." Terry put down his drink and climbed out. He turned back around. "I'll see you in a mile and we'll continue our conversation then."

Terry did a few stretches and then started up the road.

"We better get going too," Doug said.

"What about my father?" I asked. He was well up the road, still smoking.

"We'll pick him up on the way by."

Doug put the van into motion. We quickly caught up to my father, but by then Terry had already passed him. Doug pulled

over to the side of the road just ahead of my father. I opened
the door, climbed out and walked back.

"So this is pretty exciting, isn't it?" he said sarcastically.

"Not the most," I agreed.

"The only good thing is I've had some time to think."

"About what?" There was something about his expression
that made me feel hesitant.

"About you and where your life is going . . . or not going. I
hope that we can use some of this time to talk."

What more did he have to say that he hadn't said to me the
night before? Or in the van this morning? Then again, I wasn't
listening then, so I guessed I could not listen again now.

"You must be tired of just sitting there in that van and making
small talk," he said.

"You're right," I agreed.

"That's good because we could have more than small talk."
He climbed into the van.

"I'm tired of sitting in the van, so I think I'm going to run for
a while," I said.

"What?"

I *was* pretty tired of sitting in the van, and the smell was
something else. It would be good to be away from the odour.
And away from my father.

"I'll just run for a mile or so," I said. I looked at Doug. He
didn't look any more thrilled with the idea than my father did.
"Is that okay?"

He didn't answer right away. "People do sometimes run with
Terry," Doug said.

A couple of people had run a section with him earlier that day.

"Just try not to get too close," Doug said.

"What do you mean?" I asked.

"People running with Terry sometimes don't realize that his stride is different and they get tangled up. He's been knocked over a couple of times."

"I won't get that close," I promised. "I'll be careful."

Terry was way up the road already. I doubted that even if I wanted to I could catch him before the mile mark. I slammed the door of the van closed. I did a couple of stretches and then, suddenly, I felt very nervous . . . almost scared. That made no sense. What did I have to be scared about? I would run a mile. If I wanted to run more I could. If I didn't, I'd just get back in the van and pretend to listen to my father. There was nothing I could do to stop him from talking at me, but there was also nothing he could do to make me listen or talk back. I started running.

I began at a nice slow pace. My legs came up and down, slowly, the gravel crunching under my feet with each step. Within fifty yards the van passed me by, and in that split second it was passing I caught a glimpse of my father staring out the passenger window. He didn't look happy. Then again, why should now be any different than usual?

The van drove away up the highway, going wide into the left lane as it passed Terry. He was still way ahead of me, almost at the very top of the long, gradual slope that I was just starting to climb. I could feel the hill in my legs. Why hadn't I decided to start running at the top? It was too late now, though. The van had disappeared over the top and was headed downhill. Part of me wanted to just stop running and walk. Part of me wanted to dig in deeper and get to the top faster. In the end I just kept running, going no faster or slower.

Terry reached the top of the hill and disappeared over the crest, leaving me completely alone on the highway. I looked to one side and then the other: dense brush and trees. There was no telling what was in the forest—maybe bears or wolves or whatever. Maybe I *wasn't* alone. I started moving faster. I wanted to at least have Terry in sight. I could feel it in my lungs and my legs, and I was incredibly grateful when I reached the top of the hill and the road flattened out and then started going downhill.

Terry wasn't as far ahead any more. He turned around and looked at me over his shoulder. I knew that he saw me but he didn't wave or nod. He just turned back around and continued running. That same strange stride . . . over and over and over again. Was I just imagining it or was he moving faster now?

I wondered how many steps he'd taken today, and how many more steps he still had ahead of him before bed. And that was nothing. How many steps had he run since he'd left St. John's, and how many more steps before he got to the Pacific?

I heard the sound of something coming up from behind. I looked over my shoulder. It was a gigantic truck, the trailer piled high with logs. As it got closer the sound got louder and louder . . . it was barrelling down the road at a tremendous clip. I moved farther onto the shoulder and away from the blacktop. As it roared past me, I felt myself being shoved farther to the side by a gush of air, and then my face was stung by a blast of little stones and gravel as the truck thundered along the highway. Within a few seconds it came up to Terry and I saw the rush of wind push him slightly to the side.

I looked beyond Terry. The van was now parked on the side of the road. It still wasn't close—and it was at the top of *another* hill—but at least I could see how much farther I had to go before I could stop.

How could Terry do this mile after mile, day after day? What was it he said he thought about when he was running? Going home . . . running toward home . . . that was it. That didn't help me. I didn't want to think about that. The only thing worse than being at home was having to listen to my father talk about why I was having problems at home. All of last night he'd kept talking and talking and talking, and I'd just sat there listening, not knowing what to say. He kept saying he wanted answers. I would have liked some of those too. It wasn't like I knew why I kept running off and just wasn't telling him. I was still trying to figure it out myself, and the little I thought might be right didn't make any sense. It just seemed like the only time anybody noticed me was when I wasn't there.

I quickened my pace. Terry, Doug and my father were all leaning against the back bumper of the van. I was almost there, almost at the one-mile mark. I came to a stop a dozen paces behind the van and started walking.

"How did that feel?" Terry asked. He was taking a drink of water, and he didn't look half as tired as I felt.

"Okay, I guess. Those trucks can be a bit scary though," I said.

Terry smiled. "I hardly notice them any more."

"You have to be joking. I was almost blown off the road by that big lumber truck," I said.

"You just brace yourself when you hear them coming up behind you. How are your legs feeling?"

"No problem," I said.

"That's right, you used to run some cross-country."

"Yeah, last year at school."

"But not this year?"

I shook my head.

"Didn't you make the cut?" Terry asked.

"I could have made the cut," I snapped. What I didn't say was that I hadn't been allowed to try because of the problems I was having in school.

"Take it easy," Terry said. "I wasn't trying to give you a hard time. There were a few teams I made in school where nobody gave me a chance. Some people didn't think I was good enough even when I had two legs. What grade are you in?"

"Grade eight."

"You're a lot bigger than I was in grade eight. How tall are you?"

"Around five-eight."

"In grade eight I was about five-foot-nothing."

I laughed before I could stop myself, and it didn't help that I could see Doug trying to hide a grin.

"I'm glad *you* think it's funny. It was no laughing matter for me. Do you know how hard it is to make the school basketball team when you're only five feet tall?"

"It would be *impossible!*" I said.

"Not impossible. I made the team. I was a Mary Hill Cobra. It was hard, really hard. I worked my rear end off but I made it." He looked over at me. "Nothing is impossible . . . nothing." Terry took another sip of water and then handed the cup to Doug. "See you in a mile." He started up the road once again.

"You need something to drink?" Doug asked.

"Yeah, thanks."

He poured some more water into a cup and handed it to me. I took a big sip. It was cold and fresh and tasted very good going down.

"You going to run some more or ride in the van?" Doug asked.

"I thought I'd ride."

"That might be better," Doug said. "Terry usually likes to run on his own. You have to understand, he really has to concentrate pretty hard on the running. It takes a lot out of him, so he doesn't usually do much talking."

"I definitely understand that. In fact, I'm not in the mood to talk to anybody either," I said, hoping my father would get the point.

We climbed into the van and started off once again. It wasn't long before we caught up to Terry. Doug gave a slight tap on the horn as we passed by and Terry's arm shot up and he gave us a little wave. I looked back at him as we continued to drive and then leaned out the window slightly to keep him in view. Terry ran, eyes straight ahead, step after step after step. That awkward, graceful, mesmerizing gait—stride . . . skip . . . step . . . stride . . . skip . . . step. Stride after stride after stride. Mile after mile after mile. I craned my neck to keep him in view as long as I could. He finally disappeared from sight.

"Don't worry," Doug said. "You'll see him again in a little less than a mile."

"I know," I said. "It's just . . . just that it seems so strange to think that he's trying to run across the country."

"Actually," Doug said, "he isn't *trying* to run across the country . . . he *is* running across the country."

And then it hit me. What Doug had said was true. Terry wasn't talking about it, or bragging about it, he was *doing* it. And maybe he was only a little bit into the trip, but he was going to do it. One step at a time. One stride at a time. I didn't have a doubt in my mind that he was going to make it, because even if it was nearly impossible, he was going to do it. And then all at once I realized what he was staring at when he was running— he was seeing the other side of the country.

Chapter Eleven

"I'll see you in a mile," Terry said as he set off once again. That was the rhythm, repeated over and over again. Before the day was over he'd have done twenty-six miles—one mile at a time.

He started down the road. Or, more correctly, up the road—it seemed like all of Nova Scotia was on hills. Not necessarily big gigantic hills, but small, slowly rising slopes that you probably would hardly notice if you were driving a car, but you sure felt them in your legs and in your lungs when you were running. Since my run that morning I'd been noticing every one of them.

I couldn't help but wonder what it felt like for Terry. I'd run one mile. He'd run ten miles already and he was nowhere near done for the day. How could he do it? How could anybody do it?

Doug started up the van.

"Maybe this is the time for me to try to catch a few winks," my father said. He was sitting up front in the passenger seat. "Would anybody object if I just lay down in the back?"

"No problem," Doug replied.

"Change places with me," my father said. "You come up front."

My father squeezed through the seats and sat down on one of the bunks. I climbed into the front seat.

"Belt up," Doug said. I grabbed the ends and buckled up as we started to move.

I looked through the windshield. Terry was up ahead on the road, no more than a hundred yards in front of us. A car passing in the other direction slowed down and a man leaned out of the driver's window and waved. Terry, of course, waved back. We quickly caught up and Doug swung the van wide into the empty lane to pass. Terry caught sight of us out of the corner of his eye and gave another quick little wave.

"It's hard to believe that he can run twenty-six miles a day," I said.

"Day after day after day," Doug added

"Do you run?" I asked.

He nodded. Actually, he *did* look like a runner. Lean and thin, but *strong* thin.

"Did you and Terry used to run together?" I asked.

"All the time. We were on the same cross-country team, and we ran together when we were training for basketball. We played a whole lot of sports together."

"And who was better?" I asked.

Doug turned so he was partially facing me and a slight smile crossed his face. "Depends on the day, and the sport . . . and whether you asked me or Terry."

I laughed, and Doug broke into a big smile. It suddenly struck me that was the first time I'd seen him smile like that. Not that he wasn't friendly, but he just always seemed so *serious*. No, serious wasn't the right word. Watchful. No not *watchful* . . . more like *thoughtful,* like he was full of thoughts and was trying to figure things out. Or maybe he was all of those things.

"Terry and I shared the Athlete of the Year award in our senior year of high school," Doug said.

"So maybe you're about the same as athletes," I commented.

"Yeah, but you'll never get Terry to admit that . . . or me either." Again he smiled.

"How long have you and Terry been friends?"

"We first met when we were thirteen, in grade eight."

"I'm in grade eight."

"It's a good grade. A good time to be in school, don't you think?"

I didn't want to answer that question. "So you two know each other from way back. And you've been friends all along?"

He nodded. "Sometimes we went in different directions, but we've always been close. Best friends."

"That's good. It would be hard to spend all this time together with somebody who wasn't your best friend."

"It would be practically impossible," Doug agreed. "It's hard enough when it *is* your best friend."

Doug slowed the vehicle and pulled onto the gravel shoulder. "This is the mile spot. We'll wait for Terry here."

I finished off the last of my sandwich, took the garbage and tossed it into the can beside the picnic table. Doug and Terry had finished a while ago. Terry had gone into the back of the van to sleep and Doug was sitting in the passenger seat, going over some papers. He was trying to sort out the rest of the day and the plans and schedule for the days coming up. This involved where they would sleep, how far they would travel, interviews, speeches and town meetings. He did a lot more than just drive the van. I wondered if Doug was ever able to catch any sleep during the day. He obviously wasn't doing the running, but he had to be up as early as Terry every morning and probably didn't get to bed any earlier.

My father had been pacing up and down the highway. He was having trouble staying in one place and he reminded me of a caged animal. Now he wandered back to the picnic table, tossed down the butt of his cigarette and ground it into the dirt with the heel of his shoe.

"Not the most exciting way to spend a day," he said as he settled onto the bench across from me.

"Not the most."

"I didn't think this through. If I had, I would have arranged for somebody to pick us up midday. Riding in that stinky van is not my idea of fun."

"Probably a lot easier than running behind it," I said.

"But the air would certainly be fresher." He paused and gestured toward the van. "He's a pretty interesting guy."

"I guess anybody planning on running across the country would have to be pretty interesting," I commented.

"I didn't mean Terry. I was talking about Doug. What do you think of him?"

I suddenly felt like I'd been caught doing something I wasn't supposed to do, because I *had* been trying to figure him out myself. "I don't know," I mumbled.

"Come on, you must have an opinion," he said, prodding me to answer.

"Well . . . he seems nice."

"Nice? That's all you can come up with to describe him?"

I shrugged.

"You have to look at people more fully, analyze them, if you want to be a reporter," he said.

"I *never* said I wanted to be a reporter."

"You could do a lot worse than following in your old man's footsteps."

Yeah, right, footsteps that took him away from his wife and kid . . . make that his *wives and kids*. From what I knew he hadn't been any better in his first marriage than he'd been with us.

"Do you want to hear what I think?" he asked.

I knew that whether I wanted to hear or not he was going to tell me. Actually I kind of *did* want to hear what he had to say.

"First off, he's an introvert. It's his nature to be shy," he said.

That was no big news. Thanks for sharing your words of wisdom and telling me the obvious.

"Ever hear the saying 'Still waters run deep'?" my father asked.

"I've heard it, but I never really understood it."

"It means that even when the surface of the water is still and smooth there still might be a whole lot going on underneath, in the depths, where you can't see it."

"So you think Doug is deep?"

"There's a lot going on there below the surface. He's thinking. The wheels are turning."

First he's deep, still waters, and now he has wheels in his head?

"I've noticed that he's got his eyes open all the time, watching things."

"What is it that you think he's watching?" I asked.

"Anything and everything that has to do with Terry and the run. He's trying to figure things out."

My father pulled out another cigarette and lit it. The smoke drifted across the table and I shifted over to escape the noxious fumes.

"Of course," my father continued, "there's lots of things I'd like to ask Doug, but there's no point."

"Why not?"

"Two reasons. First, just because he's figured something out doesn't mean he'll tell you what he thinks. He's smart enough to keep his opinions to himself. And second, I think there are probably a lot of things—about what he's doing, about himself—that he hasn't figured out yet."

"And you have?" I questioned.

My father exhaled a cloud of smoke and nodded. That was so like him, always thinking he knew things that other people didn't.

"Why would you know something about Doug that he doesn't know about himself?" I questioned.

"Because he's just a kid . . . they both are."

"No they're not!" I protested. "They're both twenty-one or twenty-two!"

My father chuckled—a smug, self-satisfied sound. "Like I said . . ."

"So what is it that you *think* you know about Doug?"

"I think I understand something about the role he's playing in all this, how important it is. He's doing a lot more than he probably knows."

"What do you mean?" I asked.

My father stood up. "Doug and Terry are friends."

"Best friends," I said.

"And it was that friendship that brought Doug here, to drive the van. That's what he signed on to do."

"That's what he does . . . that and arrange things."

"That's right, but he's become more than that. He's become Terry's protector—that's why he's always watching—and his confidant, and his mother and his father and everything else. Terry may be out there running by himself, but he's never alone. Doug is with him all the way, every step."

My father stood up and circled around behind me. He tossed his cigarette to the ground.

"Do you have a good friend?" he asked.

"I have friends. Lots of friends."

My father nodded his head. "That's nice to know. I have friends too . . . not as many as I used to think, but I have friends." He paused. "But I know I don't have one friend who would give up half a year of his life or more to take care of me, to help me chase one of my dreams. Do you have a friend who would do that?"

I thought about what he said before answering. He was right, that was what Doug was doing. I shook my head. I didn't have a friend like that.

"That's not surprising. I don't even know if I *know* anybody who has a friend like that." He paused. "Think about it. Out of pure friendship he came along on this trip. Now, I just hope that their friendship is strong enough to survive."

"They're *best* friends," I repeated.

"Even the best of friendships can be tested, and I can only hope that friendship can survive what this journey—this quest—is going to become. Because Terry's determination, his dream, is what keeps him going. But it's Doug who's smoothing the way."

Chapter Twelve

I WALKED OVER and turned the dial on the TV. The bad, snowy image gave way to complete static. I flicked the dial to the next station—more static. I flicked it again and again and again, all with the same result. Or I guess the same *lack* of result. Lots of static and no picture. I spun it right around the dial until I arrived back at the channel where I'd originally started. It was an awful black-and-white, snow-filled image of an old, equally awful movie. I smacked the off button and the picture flickered, faded and then went dark.

I flopped onto the bed and the springs groaned under my weight. The quality of the bed was obviously a match for the quality of the TV. I checked my watch. It was only nine-thirty. Despite having gotten up at four-thirty in the morning, I still didn't feel tired enough to go to sleep. But what else was there to do? The TV was useless, there was no radio, and even if there had been one, the stations around here seemed to play only country and western music or Frank Sinatra. And, of course, since the motel was in the middle of nowhere it wasn't like there was any place for me to go.

Maybe I should have gone with my father. I didn't know exactly where he was but there had to be more action there than here. He'd left about an hour ago, saying he was going to check out a "lead" for the story. I'd figured he wasn't checking out anything more exciting than some more of his old drinking buddies, so when he invited me to go along with him I knew he really didn't mean it. Not that he'd said anything, but I could just tell by the way he asked the question and that look of relief in his eyes when I said I didn't want to come. He took off in a hurry and told me not to wait up.

Outside the room I could hear the occasional roar of a truck's engine and the *swoosh* as it zipped past us along the Trans-Canada. For a split second I thought about going out to the highway and sticking out my thumb and . . . that made no sense, and I knew it. I was hundreds and hundreds of miles away from home. There was no way I was going to run away from here. Being on the run in Toronto was one thing, but being on the run in the middle of nowhere in the middle of Nova Scotia was something else.

Then again, it wouldn't hurt to just go outside and stretch my legs. It would be good to get some fresh air into my lungs. The room smelled bad: a combination of the dozen or so cigarettes my father had smoked before he left—the butts were all smushed in the ashtray on top of the dresser—and a damp, musty odour that seemed to be oozing out of the walls. At least it didn't smell as bad as the van.

I climbed off the bed and grabbed the key from the top of the dresser. I figured I should lock the room up, even though the only thing worth stealing was my father's portable type-writer. Boy, would it tick him off if that disappeared. Somehow the thought amused me and I played with the idea in my head—but I just couldn't do that to him. I clicked the lock on as I left.

The night air felt cool and clean. I took a deep breath to replace the foul, stale air in my lungs and started to circle around to the front of the motel. Most of the units appeared to be vacant. There were no lights on in any of the windows. There were only five or six cars, plus Doug and Terry's van sitting in front of the corner unit. Either the place was practically deserted or a lot of people were out, just like my father.

As I walked I glanced anxiously at the dense forest that sat at the back of the motel. Just like when I was running along the highway, I couldn't help thinking about what might be lurking just behind that first layer of trees. Maybe Toronto had its share of dangerous things, but bears and wolves weren't high on the list.

Reaching the front of the motel I felt safer. There were a couple of lights illuminating the dirt-and-gravel parking lot. The motel sign—both the "T" and "L" only half lit—gave off a bit more light. There was also a glowing "Vacancy" sign. I wondered if the "No" part of the sign had ever been lit up.

I caught sight of headlights coming down the highway. I wondered if it could be my father . . . no, he'd said he'd be home late. The lights got bigger and bigger and the sound grew louder until it was obvious it wasn't anybody's car. A gigantic transport truck thundered by. It looked like it was going a hundred miles an hour. I tried to figure out how many hours it would take to get back to Toronto if I hitched a ride in one of those things.

Again, I pushed that thought out of my mind. I wasn't going anywhere . . . at least not right now.

I walked across the parking lot, the gravel crunching under my feet. Up above, the clouds were scattered about and the bright moon and about a million stars beamed down at me. It was amazing how many stars they had here . . . of course, we had the same number of stars back home, you just couldn't see them. It looked like tomorrow would be clear and dry at least. During the afternoon, the sky had opened and it had poured down rain for hours. Terry had been soaked to the bone. If it had been me out there running, I would have taken shelter until the rain stopped. But he wasn't me . . . I could never do what he was doing.

Off to the side of the parking lot, just over from one of the lights, stood a pole with a backboard and a hoop attached to it. I walked over. It was an old wooden board with a rusty metal rim holding the remnants of a torn and tattered mesh. The rim was bent down slightly, like somebody had been hanging on it. It wasn't much of a net, but if I'd had a ball I could at least have killed some time taking a few shots.

I was beginning to think maybe it would be better if I just went back to my room and tried to get to sleep and—I caught sight of a basketball! It was sitting in the middle of a puddle. I walked over, bent down, grabbed it and gave it a little shake to shed the water so it wouldn't soak me.

Besides being cold and wet, the ball was almost worn bald. Whoever had been using it had pretty much used it up. I spun it around. Somehow it felt like it wasn't quite round. When I bounced it, it gave off that familiar *ping* sound that basketballs make. Well, maybe it wasn't perfect but at least it could bounce. I dribbled the ball, trying to put it through my legs, but it hit an uneven spot and shot off to the side and away from me. I chased it down and grabbed it just before it rolled into another puddle. Maybe shooting would work better than dribbling.

I walked over and stood at the spot where a foul line would have been if I'd been on a real court instead of a dirt-and-gravel parking lot. I put up a shot. It hit the backboard with a loud crash and then rattled around the hoop before it fell off and bounced back to me. At least the net, backboard, ball and court were all a matching set. I put up another shot. This one swooshed in, just skimming the rim and then ruffling the tattered netting before dropping to the ground below. I gathered up the ball. I figured that was the key to this net—don't hit anything except the air in the middle of the hoop.

I dribbled out to the left side. This part of the parking lot appeared to be smoother, with only a couple of smaller puddles. I put up another shot and it banked noisily off the backboard. There was an interesting combination of sounds with the *ping* of the ball against the ground and the loud crash when it hit the backboard. I deliberately slammed the ball up against the backboard as hard as I could. The crash was like thunder, and it echoed off the motel walls.

I dribbled back to the pretend foul line. I'd play a game of twenty-one against myself, counting my shots. I spun the ball in my hands, bounced it against the ground and then put up a shot—a shot that fell well short of the rim and splashed into a puddle behind the net.

"That was one godawful shot."

I spun around. It was Terry! He was wearing his track pants and a ratty old sweatshirt, and with his hair mussed up he looked like he'd just rolled out of bed.

"Do you normally shoot that badly?" he asked.

"No, of course not!" I protested. "It was the ball, and the net and—"

"Sounds like lots of excuses. Go get it."

I ran over and picked the ball up again, shaking away the excess water.

"Pass," Terry said, holding up his hands in front of him.

I whipped over a chest pass and he caught it. He held the ball up in one hand and examined it closely. "You're right, this isn't much of a ball."

"That's what I said. If it was a good ball then—"

He put up a shot and it sailed right into the hoop, cutting me off in mid-excuse.

I grabbed the ball, and he held up his hands like he wanted me to pass again. Even in the dim light I couldn't help but see a smirk on his face. I passed him the ball. He lined up a shot and for the second time it dropped right in. I corralled the rebound and again he held out his hands.

"Pass."

For a third time I sent him a pass. This one had a little bit too much force and was off target. He had to jump to the side to catch it and he teetered, looking like he was going to fall before he regained his balance.

"You know, it's a poor workman who blames his tools," Terry said.

"What does that mean?"

"You never heard that saying before?"

I shook my head.

"It means if it doesn't drop don't blame the ball, blame the person throwing the ball." He put up another shot and this time it hit the rim and bounced up into the air and wide of the target.

"What's with that rim!" he snapped. "That shot would have dropped for sure if it was a halfway decent . . ." He stopped himself and started to laugh. "Remember, never blame the ball, but blaming the rim is okay."

I grabbed the loose ball and fed him out another pass.

"I missed. You shoot till *you* miss," he said as he returned the pass to me.

I put up a shot that didn't drop but at least hit the backboard and rim. Missing wasn't good, but at least I hadn't thrown up another brick. The ball bounced over to Terry. He aimed and the shot dropped. I snatched the ball and sent him out another pass.

"I thought you'd be asleep by now," I said.

"I should be. Four-thirty comes real soon. In fact I *was* asleep." He put up a shot that missed. "I got woken up by something."

Well, that explained his appearance—he *had* just rolled out of bed! I took the ball and walked over to a place only about six feet from the net. I wanted to make at least one shot.

"Those trucks can be pretty loud as they barrel by here," I said. I put up the shot and mercifully it dropped.

"It wasn't the trucks," he said as he got the rebound and tossed it to me.

"If it wasn't the trucks then what was it that. . . ?" Instantly I knew the answer to my question. It was me playing basketball.

"But that's okay. It's been a while since I played some ball. It's one of my favourite sports," he said. "Do you want to have a game?"

"You mean like twenty-one or something like that?" I asked.

"No offence but I *know* the way I shoot and I've *seen* the way you shoot. It wouldn't be much of a contest. I was thinking more about a game."

"You want to play me one on one?" I asked in disbelief.

"I don't see anybody else around here," he replied. "Of course, you could just smash a few more shots against the backboard and maybe we could wake up a couple more guys." He laughed. "Let's just play a little ball."

"But will that be okay?"

He shrugged. "I'm bigger, taller, stronger, more experienced and have a better shot. You've got two legs. Sounds about even to me. You want first ball?"

"No," I said, shaking my head. "You can start with it."

"Suit yourself," he said as he took the ball from my hands. "It might be the last time you ever see the ball, though. I used to play for the Junior Varsity team at Simon Fraser University."

"They have a wheelchair team?" I asked.

"Regular team, regular ball . . . before this," he said, touching his artificial leg.

I suddenly felt bad for mentioning it. It wasn't like we both didn't know that he had a missing leg, but still, I didn't like bringing it up.

"Check," he said and tossed me the ball. I tossed it back. Before I could even think to react he'd squared up to the net, put the ball up and it dropped for a basket.

"That makes one. How about game is ten baskets?"

"Sure, that's fine," I said as I grabbed the loose ball.

"And we better make it that the other person gets the ball after a basket," he said.

"Okay, that's——"

"That way you'll at least get to hold the ball a couple of times," he said and laughed.

Funny, really funny.

I starting dribbling, and Terry came out on me. I faked one way, went the other, and just as I was going by he reached out, smashing the ball and my hand!

"Hey, foul!" I screamed as he scrambled after the loose ball.

"Foul?" He grabbed the ball and looked over at me. "You call that a foul?"

"You hit my hand!" I protested.

"I hit your hand *on* the ball. That makes it part of the ball. You here to complain or play basketball?"

"Play ball."

"Then you better cover me or I'm going to go up two baskets to zip."

I walked over and put myself between him and the basket just as he put up a shot. It clanked off the backboard, spun around the rim and dropped.

"I was hoping this would be a game," he said. "If you're not going to come up and cover me you might as well go back to your room."

His tone of voice, the sort of taunting quality, was starting to get on my nerves. If he wanted a game I'd give him a game.

I took the ball and started dribbling. Terry reached in to try to knock it away again. I spun around so I was backing into him. I faked one way, then the other, and as he lunged forward we bumped together! I turned the corner on him while he stumbled backwards! I went up for an easy layup!

"That makes it two baskets to one and—" I stopped mid-sentence. Terry was on the ground, sitting in a puddle.

"I'm so sorry!" I exclaimed.

"Don't be sorry," he said. "You made the basket."

"I didn't mean to knock you over." I rushed over and offered him my hand to get up.

"It was a good play. No foul." He took my hand and I pulled him to his feet.

"My ball. Now let's see if you can stop me."

Terry began dribbling. I had expected him to just take another shot. He moved over to the side. His dribbling had the same strange awkwardness as his run. I jumped forward, trying to separate him from the ball. We bumped together. For a split second I thought we were both going to tumble over, but we both regained our balance, and as I backed off a half step he moved around me and put up an easy layup for his third basket.

"You should play to win. *I'm* playing to win. Come on, Winston, don't back off," Terry said.

"I was afraid I was going to knock you over again," I explained.

"And if you did?" he asked with a shrug. "I'd just get back up again. If you haven't noticed, I'm pretty hard to keep down . . . or beat. Your ball," he said as he tossed it to me. "Try your hardest to score, 'cause believe me, *I'm* going to try my hardest to stop you." He paused and a big smile crossed his face. "Now let's play some ball."

Chapter Thirteen

"You going to finish those?" Terry asked, pointing to the last of the fries on my plate.

"No, I don't think—" He reached over and grabbed my plate. "—I'm going to finish them."

"Thanks," he mumbled, and he stuffed a couple of the fries into his mouth. "I'm still hungry."

"How can you be hungry?" I asked in disbelief.

"I really work up an appetite out there on the road."

An appetite was one thing, but the way he could pack it away was another thing entirely. He'd already eaten two cheeseburgers, a large order of fries, a huge hunk of apple pie topped with ice cream and a gigantic salad, and washed it all down with a chocolate milkshake.

"In Newfoundland I had a waitress watch me eat and she asked me if I had a hollow leg," Terry said.

I laughed.

"I told her it was actually metal and fibreglass."

Doug chuckled and Terry broke into a big, goofy sort of grin. That was good to see, because so far I hadn't seen either of them smile that whole morning. They hadn't been talking, either. Okay, maybe a couple of words, but it was like they weren't saying anything they didn't really, really need to say. At first I just figured they were too tired or busy to talk. But by the time lunch came rolling around it was pretty obvious that they were fighting. Maybe fighting wasn't the right word, because they weren't arguing or even disagreeing. It was more like they were pretending that the other one wasn't there. This is not the easiest thing to do when you're inside a little van, no more than ten feet away from the other person. When Terry came in from a run, Doug would sometimes climb out of the van. When they were both sitting in there I could practically smell the tension—that and the portable toilet. And what was up with that toilet? The van never smelled good, but today it just reeked. It made me want to gag.

"Do you have time for a few questions?" a woman asked. She wore a little badge around her neck that identified her as being from a newspaper.

"Sure," Terry said. "Have a seat."

"You can have mine," Doug said as he rose to his feet. "I've got some phone calls to make."

"You always seem to be doing something," the woman offered.

"*Always something,*" Doug said, emphasizing both words.

"I should go too," I said.

I got up and strolled across the restaurant. My father was sitting at a table at the very back. I'd actually wanted to eat lunch with him. I'd been riding in the van all morning and I hadn't seen him at all because he was driving a rental car. But when I'd said I was going to eat with him both Doug and Terry had insisted that I join them for lunch instead. I think the invitation had less to do with my company, or my uneaten french fries, than it had to do with them just wanting somebody else around so there'd be some conversation.

"How you doing?" I asked as I plopped down on the bench across from my father in the booth.

"Not great. Working on my story."

"Isn't it going well?" I asked.

He shook his head. "I've got a few ideas, but it's hard with all these other reporters around."

"There certainly are a lot more. Even more than yesterday."

"They get in the way," he said. "And do you know what's even worse than a bad reporter?"

"A lot of bad reporters?" I asked.

He laughed. "No, a lot of *good* reporters."

"How can that be worse?"

"Because good reporters write good stories. Have you read any of these articles?" he asked, gesturing to newspapers scattered across the table in front of him.

"I haven't seen a newspaper in days. Besides, the only things I read are the sports and the comics."

"There's this one by Christie Blatchford, and another one by Leslie Scrivener." He shook his head.

"They wrote bad articles?" I asked.

"I wish they had. They both wrote *great* articles."

"And that's bad?"

"Bad for me. You know, there are only so many stories, so many angles to cover any event, and it makes my job harder when other people are covering those angles." Again he shook his head. "There were no female reporters in my day," he muttered.

"I thought *this* was your day," I said.

"My *early* days. Back when I started, no self-respecting woman would even dream of becoming a—"

"You mean like my mother?" I challenged.

"You know what I mean. Your mother wasn't a reporter when I started."

"That's right. Was she even *born* when you started?"

He shot me a dirty look. "Besides, your mother isn't a reporter, she's a news producer, a *TV* news producer. And speaking of your mother, I was talking to my editor today and he told me your mother had called him because she wanted to get in contact with us. She told him she hadn't heard from us." He fixed me with an accusing gaze. "You'll call her, tonight, right?"

I shrugged. "Sure, whatever."

"I know you're mad at her, but that doesn't mean you can just ignore her. It's only fair that you call and—"

"The way you called when you first left us?" I snapped.

My father put down the paper he was holding. What was he going to say to that?

"I deserved that," he said. "And you didn't deserve me not calling. What I did wasn't fair, and believe me, I'm sorry. Just, please don't do something to your mother that you know was hurtful to you . . . okay?"

Now I didn't know what to say. I was looking for a fight and he wasn't giving me one.

"Tell you what, I'll make the call tonight when we get to the hotel. I'll tell her it's my fault that nobody called. She's used to things being my fault so she'll believe it for sure," he said, and then he laughed.

I nodded. "You're right—she'll have no trouble buying that."

"But that doesn't take care of my bigger problem. What am I going to write about today? I have to have something filed by nine this evening if it's going to be in tomorrow's paper."

"That's lots of time."

"It's lots of time when you have a story idea, but I'm coming up empty. I've never missed a deadline in my life and I'm not about to start now."

"There must be *something* to write about," I said. I knew that really wasn't very helpful, but it wasn't my business to help him do his job, either.

"Nothing much has happened today. What am I supposed to write—Terry's still running?"

"Well, he is," I said.

"Maybe he is, but that's not *new,* and it's not called a *news-* paper for nothing. The public gets tired of reading about the same things every day. And the ironic thing is that each day he runs, the running becomes less significant."

"Shouldn't it be *more* significant?" I protested.

"Not really. The public has a very short attention span, even for things as important as wars, so how long do you think they're going to want to read about Terry running another day?"

"They should want to read about it. What he's doing is important!" I argued.

"Ah, but that's what you don't understand. There's a big difference between *important* and *newsworthy.*"

"You lost me."

"There are many incredibly important things happening in the world every day. Meetings between world leaders. Scientists making medical breakthroughs. But that doesn't mean that those things are newsworthy. You're not the only one who goes straight to the comics and the sports section. Newspapers want news that sells papers. Ever heard the saying 'It's the sizzle that sells the steak'?"

I shook my head. He was a wealth of old sayings . . . I figured that was because he was old.

"It means something has to have a buzz to it, be exciting, to capture the public's attention."

"But this story did get their attention. All those phone calls you got . . . and it brought other reporters."

"I didn't say it didn't get their attention. The question is, how long can it *hold* their attention? Of course, what will help keep their attention is pictures, either on TV or in the papers. That's why I have a photographer joining us. I think I'm going to have him get some shots of Terry running up a steep hill—his expression looks so strained, like he's in pain. Do you think he's in much pain?"

"I think it hurts. It has to."

My father pulled out a cigarette from the package on the table. He flicked his lighter and lit up.

"Do you remember when I mentioned how big it would be if somebody found out that Terry wasn't really running the whole way?" my father asked.

"Of course I do . . . but you know that isn't true! You know how carefully they mark the spot, and how Terry steps right on the plastic bag, and about the time it blew away and he ran an extra three miles so—"

"I know, I know," he said.

"You almost sound disappointed."

"Not disappointed. I'm just saying it would be a big story. It's like I said, the only thing the public likes better than building up a hero is tearing him down."

"You're wrong, people don't want him to fail."

"That's true, they don't *want* Terry to fail, but if he did they'd read every story about it. Bad news sells."

"And if you found out something bad about Terry, you'd write about it?"

He shrugged. "If it was the truth. Truth is what the business is all about. I'd be *obligated* to write about it."

"But what if you got your information wrong? Newspapers make mistakes all the time. I'm always reading those little apology things they print. What do you call those?"

"Retractions."

"Yeah, retractions. It's like there's one of those in every paper I've ever read."

"I thought you only read the comics and the sports section," he said.

"I read other stuff, sometimes. What if you wrote something about Terry and you got it wrong, you made a mistake?"

"Then there'd be an apology the next day."

"Have you ever made a mistake?" I paused. "I mean, with a story." I hoped he got that dig.

"I've made more than my fair share of mistakes . . . with stories and with life. I guess the important thing is to admit you were wrong and try to do better in the future."

For a split second I thought I saw—or just really wanted to see—my father's eyes glistening. Was he going to tell me he was sorry, was he going to apologize for leaving us . . . or had he just done that?

"We all make mistakes," I said, breaking the silence. Maybe I'd just said "It's okay" to him.

"You know, you can help make sure I don't make mistakes with this story," he said.

"I can?"

"Yes. I'd like you to read every article I write before I send it. The way you did with the first one. And if you see something you think is wrong, you tell me."

"And you'll change it?" I asked.

"And we'll talk about it. If you can convince me it's wrong then I'll change it. But do you know what you can do that would be even more of a help?"

"What?"

"Keep your eyes and ears open."

"What do you mean?"

"You're spending a lot of time with Doug and Terry. You see and hear things that the rest of us don't get to see and hear. They're pretty guarded when they're talking with reporters, but not with you. For example, the other day when we were riding in the van and I went into the back to lie down, I heard you and Doug talking."

"You were eavesdropping on us?"

"Not eavesdropping. I couldn't help but listen. It's a little van."

Okay, maybe he had a point.

"And I noticed that Doug is much more open when he's around you. Terry is the same way. They've already become cautious around the press—and that's probably wise. But with you they seem more comfortable. For example, what do you and Terry talk about when I'm not around?"

"Nothing really," I said defensively. "Mostly just about sports."

"Well, if he said anything different then you could tell me about it."

"So you're saying you want me to spy on them?" I asked in disbelief.

"Not spy. Report. Just tell me things. That's what a reporter does, sees and hears things and then writes about them."

"It still sounds like spying."

"It's not spying. Besides, it would help Terry."

"How would it help Terry?" This was all making me more than a bit suspicious.

"It would help because he's trying to raise money for cancer research, and the more interesting an article is, the more attention it will get. And the more attention it gets, the more money will be raised. Do you see the connection?"

"I guess I do."

"Good. Then can you do that to help me?"

I didn't know what to answer. I just knew that even if what he said was right, it still left a bad taste in my mouth.

"All I want is for you to keep your eyes and ears open. Can you do that?"

Slowly I nodded my head. I could keep my eyes and ears open. I could also keep my mouth shut if it seemed like the right thing to do.

"I don't mean you're looking for bad things. I just mean interesting things. Human interest items. You know, what sort of music they like . . . things like that. It would really help. It's becoming harder to keep this thing interesting with each passing day. This story won't become really big until he stops running."

"The Pacific Ocean is a long way from here," I said.

"The Pacific is, but the end of the run might not be."

"What do you mean?" Did he know something that I didn't know? Was Terry getting ready to abandon the run for some reason?

"It's just that you have to understand what it is that Terry's trying to do," he said.

"I understand exactly what he's doing!" I snapped. "He's running across Canada to raise money for cancer research!"

"He's running across the country on one leg."

"I sort of noticed that!"

He ignored my jab. "Running twenty-six miles even once is an incredible accomplishment. Something that only a few thousand people in the whole country have ever done. But he's running a marathon today, and he's going to do the same thing tomorrow and the next day and the next. Just like he did the day before and the day before that and the day before that."

"I know that!" I snapped.

"And he's going to have to do that for close to two hundred days."

Two hundred days . . . wow . . . I hadn't thought about just how many days it was going to take.

"And he's doing it on *one* leg, after having cancer and all the treatment that goes with it. Do you have any idea just how incredible this all is? Nobody has ever attempted anything like this . . . ever."

I let his words sink in. Everything he had said made sense. Perfect sense. I felt a lump growing in my stomach.

"I know you like Terry—heck, *I* like Terry. He's almost impossible not to like. It's just that I don't want you to get your hopes too high. The higher you get, the more it hurts when you fall. What he's trying to do is nearly impossible."

"Nearly impossible?" I asked.

He nodded his head.

"But not *completely* impossible," I said.

"Not completely."

I got up from the table. "He's going to do it."

Across the room I saw Terry get up to leave. "I better get going. I think I'm going to ask if I can travel in the van again this afternoon."

Chapter Fourteen

BY THE TIME I got to the door of the restaurant Terry was already outside and getting ready to climb into the van.

"Hey, is it okay if I ride along with you guys again?" I yelled.

He smiled and motioned for me to get in. I ran over and got into the passenger seat as Terry climbed into the back. I did up my seatbelt and Doug started to drive away.

Terry poked his head between the seats. "Good to have you along."

"It's good to be along." Although it really, really smelled bad. I rolled down my window to let in a little fresh air.

"Do you know what the road looks like up ahead?"

"Black . . . yellow line down the middle, lots of gravel along both sides," Terry said and then chuckled.

"I meant is it hilly?"

"This whole country is on a hill," Terry said. "I'm not sure why everybody in Canada doesn't just roll down to one of the oceans."

I laughed.

"I think there's a flat spot somewhere on the prairies," he continued. "Then everything will be downhill from there . . . except for the mountains."

Doug pulled the van off the blacktop and onto the gravel. He slowed down, cruising along the shoulder. I knew what he was looking for. There it was up ahead, a plastic bag weighed down with rocks and gravel—the exact spot where Terry had stopped running before lunch. Doug slowed the van to a crawl and then brought it to a stop right beside the marker.

"I think this might be my stop," Terry said. He opened the sliding side door and I watched as he put his foot down right on top of the bag. That was the way he always did it. He never cheated by even an inch, and anybody who even thought about writing a story like that was nothing more than a stinking liar!

Terry stretched. Doug stayed behind the wheel of the van. He was studying some papers, probably sorting out the rest of the day. I climbed out as well and looked up ahead. There was a hill directly in front of us, another one of those long, slow inclines. This one gradually rose up until it twisted around a corner, so you couldn't even see where it ended. According to what Terry had told me it ended somewhere in Saskatchewan.

"I'll see you two in a mile." Terry started running.

I walked around to the front of the van and sort of leaned against the bumper and watched him. As always there was something about the way he ran—a step, skip and a stride with the artificial leg—that was hard not to watch. I'd never seen anything that was so awkward and so graceful at the same time.

Up ahead, almost like magic, some people appeared on the side of the road. They hadn't driven up so they must have come out of the houses that were scattered along the highway. As Terry passed they began to clap and cheer, and somebody reached out to offer him something—probably a donation. People had been continually pressing money into Terry's hands or passing it through the window to Doug—all going to fight cancer. More and more people each day, all of them having heard about Terry and wanting to contribute to the Marathon of Hope.

I'd seen this same thing happen in one form or another at least twenty times over the past few days, but it still amazed me—strangers standing on the highway cheering on this person they didn't know. And I knew it had been happening more today than yesterday. My father was wrong. People weren't getting tired of this run, they were getting more enthusiastic about it, and it would get bigger and bigger with each passing day.

I circled around and climbed back into the van. The odour hit me like a wave.

"I'd forgotten about the smell," I said.

"It's pretty hard to forget . . . or ignore," Doug said.

"It's the toilet, right?" I asked.

"Yep," Doug said without looking up from his papers.

"You really have to do something about that."

"*Somebody* has to do something about it. *Somebody* has to clean it out."

"Somebody?"

He put the papers down and looked at me. "I've been taking care of it all along. Now I'm too busy doing all these other jobs. Besides arranging places to stay and interviews and scheduling appearances, who do you think buys the groceries and does the laundry? So maybe it's *somebody else's* turn to empty the holding tank."

"But there's only you and Terry," I said.

"Then I guess it's his turn. Terry's the one who fills it, so maybe he should be the one who empties it."

I knew they had been fighting. I guess my father was right to worry about the strain on their friendship—it looked like it might be busting up over something pretty stupid.

"Is it hard to do, cleaning out the holding tank?" I asked.

"Not hard. Doesn't take long. Just a few minutes." Doug put his papers down beside the seat and started up the van again. He looked in the side-view mirror and, seeing that it was clear, pulled out.

"You know," I said, thinking through my words, not believing that I was actually going to say what I was going to say, "if some-body showed me how, I could take care of it."

"You?"

I nodded.

Doug looked over at me. "Thanks for offering, man, but you didn't fill it either." He paused. "You're only here for a few days. It's one of those things that Terry and I have to work out between us."

I felt relief.

"And Winston . . . we *will* work it out, don't worry."

As we caught up to Terry I could see that he wasn't alone. There were four other people running with him. I guess whether he wanted it or not he was going to get more and more company. The cars up ahead of us slowed down and people honked their horns and waved as they passed. That had been happening a lot more today as well. We went wide around Terry and the other runners and I waved out the window. Terry gave a little wave in reply. I think he was waving to both of us.

"I noticed you have a tape player in the van," I said. "Could we listen to a little music?"

"Sure," Doug said. He reached over and pushed in a tape that was sticking partway out. There was a click, a hiss, and then the van was filled with the sound of twangy guitars and a rough, raw voice.

"Who is this?" I demanded.

"Johnny Cash. He's one of Terry's favourite singers."

"You've got to be joking."

"Don't you like him?" Doug asked.

I snorted in reply.

"Terry's brother Darrell made the tape for us. It's the best of Johnny Cash."

"Must be an awfully short tape."

Doug reached over and turned down the volume. "Have a look at the other tapes. We must have something that you'd like better."

I rummaged through a box sitting on the floor between the seats. There were lots of tapes . . . more Johnny Cash . . . the Everly Brothers . . . some gospel tapes . . . Hank Williams . . . Dolly Parton, at least she was good to *look* at.

"See anything you like?" Doug asked.

I shook my head.

"Then I guess we'll just keep listening to Johnny."

For the first time in my life I think I would have been happy to have heard from the Chairman of the Board . . . Mr. Frank Sinatra.

"So, are you planning on doing any running today?" Terry asked me.

I didn't answer right away. I'd been thinking it would be nice to run a couple of miles—to stretch my legs and get away from the smell in the van—but I knew Terry liked to run by himself.

"Well?" he asked.

"I guess I'll just ride in the van," I finally answered.

"That's too bad," Terry said. "I was hoping you'd keep me company for a couple of miles."

"What?" I couldn't believe my ears.

"You *want* him to run with you?" Doug asked. He sounded just as surprised by what Terry had said as I was.

"I was just thinking that it would be nice to have a little company," Terry said, shrugging his shoulders.

"I could run with you . . . if you want me to."

"If I didn't, I wouldn't have asked. You want to run this section?"

"Sure . . . I could . . . I guess. But I thought you liked it better when you got to run alone."

"Most of the time it is better . . . easier. And I especially like to be by myself in the mornings. I like the quiet . . . it gives me time to think. Other times I actually like having company. And sometimes it seems like I don't have any choice, people just tag along."

"I noticed. Especially today."

"It's getting to be more people all the time. That's okay now and again, but I do need to concentrate. And sometimes people run too close. I almost got tripped twice today. And there's always a lot of questions. I know people are just being friendly and curious, but I really need to save my lungs for running, not for answering questions."

"I'll try not to ask questions," I said. "Except maybe to ask you to *slow down* a little when we're going up the hills."

Terry laughed, and I laughed along with him. He had the kind of laugh that made you want to join in.

"Let's get started," he said.

"See you gentlemen in a mile," Doug called out.

We started running. I kept way over to the side and ran well behind Terry. We ran along in silence. There was no noise except for our feet hitting the road and gravel. The silence was broken occasionally by the *whoosh* of passing cars and people tapping on their horns or yelling encouragement out their windows.

Terry looked back over his shoulder. "You can run a little bit closer than that if you want."

"Sure," I said. I moved up a bit.

"And you can talk to me, it's okay," he added.

"Sure . . . I just didn't want to bother you."

"That's all right, don't worry about it."

I moved up closer but made sure there was no way I was close enough to get tripped up in his feet. He'd said we could talk and there was something that I was curious about.

"Do you mind if I ask you one question?"

"No problem . . . as long as you don't try to trip me."

"I was just wondering . . . does it hurt when you run?"

"Not really," he said.

"It doesn't?"

"It hurts sometimes," he admitted.

"Does it hurt today?"

"Sometimes."

"What do you mean *sometimes*?" I persisted.

"Sometimes the stump hurts, but only when I put pressure on it."

"What sort of pressure?"

He didn't answer right away. Maybe because my one question had become a lot of questions he wasn't going to answer.

"It only hurts when I run on it."

"But you're *always* running on it!" I exclaimed.

"Not always . . . just every second step," he said, and smiled.

"That's awful. If it hurts you have to do something."

"What?" he asked. "Here's what I can do. I can stop running, I can hop on one leg, or I can just keep going and put up with it . . . not much of a choice, really, is it?"

"Does Doug know that it hurts?"

"Doug knows everything. He's the *only* one who knows . . . except, I guess, for you now. And you have to promise me you won't tell anybody."

"I won't."

"Not even your father."

"Not even anybody."

"I just don't want people making it into a big deal. I don't want them feeling sorry for me."

"I won't tell anybody. I promise."

We continued to run along in silence. I was now much more aware of his artificial leg hitting the ground. With each step, each single step, it caused him pain. How could he keep doing that?

"Does it hurt a lot?" I asked, knowing I should shut up but needing to know.

"It's more of an ache than a pain," he said. "Sort of like stubbing your toe . . . a few thousand times a day."

Just at the top of the hill I could see the van. Doug was sitting on the back bumper, looking back at us. He waved and I waved back.

"It must be nice to have a friend like that," I said.

"It is . . . and even when we're not talking to each other—I guess you've noticed—we're still best friends. We've been friends for a long time and we've had fights for a long time. Sometimes he gets on my nerves and sometimes I get on his. Doesn't mean anything."

Terry continued to run but I slowed down to a walk about fifty yards from the van. Somehow that just seemed like the thing to do. Doug offered Terry a cup of water and he sat down on the bumper beside him. Doug was holding a plate of cut-up oranges. They were talking. That was nice to see.

Another section was over. Terry was one mile closer to the Pacific. One mile closer to the run being over. One mile closer to being home.

As I came up to the van Terry and Doug were talking and joking around. That brought a smile to my face and—I stopped dead in my tracks. There were red streaks running down Terry's artificial leg—it looked like blood!

I gasped and brought my hand up to point at Terry's leg. He looked up at me and then down—there were two little red trickles rolling down the side of his prosthesis. Terry scowled and muttered something under his breath.

"You're . . . you're . . ."

"I'm bleeding."

"Bleeding!" I exclaimed. "You're hurt!"

"I'm bleeding, but I'm not hurt."

Doug handed me the plate holding the rest of the oranges. "I'll get you a towel," he offered, and he climbed into the van. He quickly returned with a white towel that he handed to Terry. Terry took the towel and proceeded to wipe off his leg, removing the blood.

"It's nothing," Terry said.

"It's not nothing. It's blood," I insisted.

"It's nothing serious," he said.

"How can blood not be serious?"

"You ever had a blister on your foot?" Terry asked.

"Yeah, once, a long time ago when I had new shoes."

"And when it broke did it bleed?"

"I can't really remember that much about it but I don't think it was blood . . . more like clear stuff, like water."

"Well, I have things that are like blisters on my stump."

I tried not to shudder. I'd worked hard at not imagining the end of his leg.

"They're called cysts. They're really just sores like blisters and when they break sometimes there's a little bit of blood." He took the towel and cleared off the last trace of it. "It's really nothing."

"Maybe you should see a doctor," I said.

"There's no point," Terry replied.

"But he could tell you how to stop the sores from happening or stop them from breaking and bleeding," I suggested.

"I know how to stop them."

"Then why aren't you doing it?" I asked.

"Because the answer is that I have to rest."

"You mean like take a day off?"

"A day or two or maybe a week."

"A week? That seems like a long time. But maybe you should do that."

"I *can't* do that. Especially now. Things are starting to pick up steam. There's more notice, we're raising more money each day. I can't lose the momentum."

"But if you're in pain and you need rest to get healed then you really should stop running for a while."

"Not going to happen," Terry said. "If I stopped every time I felt a little bit of pain I'd still be somewhere in Newfoundland. Or probably I'd have given up when I was running laps and I'd still be back home. Pain is just part of it. Tired is just part of it. You have to run through those things." He paused. "But tell you what, I will take a bit of a break."

"You will?"

"Sure. I'm going to run for another mile and then I'm going to take at least a five-minute break." He smiled, got up off the bumper and disappeared around the side of the van.

"He'll be okay," Doug said quietly.

"Are you sure?"

Doug nodded. "This has been a problem for a while."

"I didn't know."

"Nobody knows. We've been trying to keep it quiet."

The hairs on the back of my neck stood up. I knew that this was exactly the sort of thing my father was looking for, an angle, something that nobody else knew.

"Terry thinks that if people knew they might think he should stop, the way *you* think he should stop."

"But if *I* saw the blood . . . other people will see it too."

"We try to be careful. Usually the blood doesn't overflow out of the cup."

"The cup?"

"The top of the prosthesis—the artificial leg—is like a cup that fits over the end of Terry's leg."

I thought back to when I'd held Terry's leg and tried to picture the cup.

"Usually the cup catches all of the leakage."

"But it didn't this time. That must mean that there's *more* blood than usual," I argued.

"This is more than usual, but it's been like this before."

"Maybe he really should go and see a doctor," I suggested again.

"That's not going to happen," Doug said. "For one thing, the doctors don't really know how to deal with Terry's problems— he's pretty much the first guy to put so much wear and tear on a leg by running. And anyway, I think Terry's seen enough doctors to last a lifetime." Doug paused. "He once told me about going down to the clinic where he was getting the cancer treatment. He told me that he'd get the shivers, and it had nothing to do with being cold."

"But if he needs to see a doctor he has to. You should make him go."

Doug smiled. "Do you really think that *anybody* could make Terry do *anything* he didn't want to do? He's as stubborn as a mule."

"You must be talking about yourself again," Terry said as he reappeared around the corner of the van.

"Compared to you I haven't got a stubborn bone in my whole body!" Doug snapped, and then they both started to laugh.

I must have looked white as a sheet because Terry said, "Winston, you worry too much. I'll be okay!"

"I just think that it wouldn't hurt to stop for a while."

"I will stop."

"You will?" I asked, and I could see from Doug's expression that I wasn't the only one shocked by what he'd just said.

"Yep. I'll stop as soon as I hit the Pacific Ocean." Terry flashed a huge smile. "See you in a mile, man," he said as he gave Doug a slap on the back and started up the road once again.

Doug just shook his head and then circled around the van. I hurried around to the other side and climbed in.

"Before we go, there's something I wanted to ask you," Doug said. "I feel bad for even mentioning it."

"Mentioning what?" I asked.

"I know you wouldn't anyway . . . but I just . . . you know . . . would really appreciate it if you didn't say anything about the bleeding to anybody. It really isn't something we want people to know about."

"I won't! I already promised Terry!" I'd also already made that decision in my mind.

Doug smiled. "I knew you wouldn't. Thanks. I appreciate it. Terry appreciates it." He started the van up. "Now we better get going. Like I've said before, it looks bad if the guy with one leg can run a mile faster than I can drive it."

Chapter Fifteen

I RODE IN THE VAN for another mile and then went back out to run with Terry again. I kept trying to catch sideways glances as he ran beside me. I wasn't looking at his stride this time, I was checking to make sure that there wasn't any blood leaking down his leg. It looked okay. I didn't see anything. I just hoped his leg was okay. I hoped *he* was okay.

"You're awfully quiet," Terry said.

"Just thinking." And trying not to pester him with questions.

"About what?"

"About school," I lied. I didn't want him to know what I'd really been thinking about.

"You said you were in grade eight, right?"

"Unfortunately."

"Not having a great year?"

I wanted to lie to him again, not tell him how things really were, but I just felt like I couldn't. "It's been a bad year. Really bad."

"So bad that you didn't want to go to school for a few days?" Terry asked.

"So bad that they won't *let* me go to school for a few days."

"Wow, suspended. What did you do?"

"It's not so much what I did, apparently it's my attitude." That was a word I'd been getting pretty sick of hearing. "Were you ever suspended?"

"Never," he said. "Good thing too. My parents would have killed me. How did your parents take it?"

"My mother was pretty upset. My father didn't know at first."

"How did you keep that from him?"

"I live with my mother . . . remember?" I said.

"Right. I just sort of forgot because you and your father are so close."

I almost laughed out loud. We weren't close at all!

"And it's just you and your mother? No brothers or sisters?" Terry asked.

"I have two brothers—well, step-brothers, or half-brothers or whatever. They're from my father's first marriage. They're older, grown-ups. Anybody else in your family?"

"An older brother, Fred, he's twenty-three, a younger brother Darrell who's seventeen and then my sister Judith. She's the baby, she's only fourteen. Your age."

"Must be nice," I said.

"It is, most of the time . . . depends on how many bathrooms you have in your house. Sometimes it would be nice to have less people or more bathrooms."

We ran along silently, just listening to the gravel crunching under our feet.

"I can't get over how big you are for grade eight," Terry said.

"I'm not that big, it's just that you were really small," I said, remembering that he'd told me he was only five feet tall. "You must have been one of the shortest kids in the whole grade," I said.

"Me and Doug."

"Doug was short too?"

"I always thought I was a hair taller than him."

"And what did Doug think?"

Terry laughed out loud. "You already know us too well! Me and Doug met on the first day of cross-country try-outs. We were the only grade eights going out for the team. Everybody else was in nine or ten."

"That must have been hard."

"Hard for the nines and tens. We finished first and second. I couldn't catch him, but he couldn't lose me."

"Doug won?"

"Doug always won. He's a really good runner."

"Yeah, he told me he did some running," I said.

"He did a little more than *some* running. In our senior year in high school he got the silver medal for cross-country. He finished second for the whole province of British Columbia. He's a great runner."

"He didn't mention that."

"Doug wouldn't. Guy doesn't like to talk about himself. He's like that . . . modest . . . quiet. And speaking of quiet, it must be awfully quiet at your place with just you and your mom living there."

"Sometimes it's too quiet . . . way too quiet."

Terry glanced over at me with a questioning look. Part of me didn't want to tell him anything, but another part knew that he really wanted to hear what I had to say.

"We fight . . . a lot . . . and when we fight we don't talk . . . sometimes for days at a time." I knew what I wanted to say next but I didn't know if I had the nerve to say it. I inhaled even more deeply through my nostrils. "You and Doug fight sometimes."

"Sometimes. I guess everybody fights sometimes."

"But you guys shouldn't fight!" I blurted out.

He didn't answer right away. "Doug's my best friend."

"That's even more reason why you shouldn't! Best friends should never fight!"

Terry started to laugh. "Do you have a best friend?"

"I've got lots of friends . . . I just wouldn't say that any one of them is really my best friend."

"There's something about being best friends that means you're *allowed* to fight," Terry said. "I've had some of my very best fights with my best friend and my brothers."

"I don't understand."

Again, Terry didn't answer right away and we just ran along in silence.

"I think the best fights are the ones you have with the people you're closest to. Me and Doug are together twenty-four hours a day, seven days a week, week after week, in either that van or a little motel room. Sooner or later we're bound to start fighting about something."

"Like you're doing now?" I asked.

Terry chuckled. "You're pretty sharp. We're not really fighting, though, we're just sort of not talking too much."

"Like me and my mother," I suggested. "I think being silent is worse than fighting with words."

"Yeah, I think you're right."

"You two have to get along. What you're doing is too important to jeopardize it by fighting," I said. "The Marathon of Hope is too important."

"We're not putting the run at risk. You have to know about the two of us—even if we're not talking, even if we're fighting, even if we're so mad we feel like strangling each other, it doesn't matter. He's *my* best friend. I'm *his* best friend. Any fight we have will end, we'll start talking again, and we'll still be best friends."

"It's not going to stop you from running?"

"Not a chance."

"Doug's not going to get so ticked off he decides to just get up and leave?"

"Even less than a chance. One thing I know about Doug is that I can depend on him. When he gives his word he'll stick by it, no matter what. I know he's somebody who won't give up." He paused. "Besides, we both know that you can't run away from your problems."

I felt like he'd just poked me with a stick. Did he know about me running away from home?

"I may be running across the entire country, but I'm not running *away* from anything. I'm running *to* something. I'm running to my home in Port Coquitlam, running to help all those people, all those kids, who can't run. I'm running to raise money to find a cure for cancer." He paused. "And Doug may be driving the van, but he's actually running every step with me . . . every step. Does that make sense?"

I nodded. "It makes a lot of sense."

We continued to run along. I thought that maybe we were both thinking through what Terry had just said.

"So, how many more days are you going to be hanging out with us?" Terry asked.

"I'm here for tomorrow for sure, and maybe a day after that."

"And then you'll go back to Toronto."

"Back home," I agreed.

"So when we get to Toronto you'll come and say hello?"

"When will you be in Toronto?"

"Sometime in July."

"Yeah, I'll be there for sure," I said.

"You know, that's one of the things I like about you."

"What?"

"You didn't even hesitate. You don't have any doubts that I'm going to make it to Toronto, do you?" Terry asked.

"Why would I?" I asked. "Isn't it between here and the Pacific Ocean?"

Terry's face broke into a big smile, and I smiled back.

Terry climbed awkwardly up onto the back of the big flatbed truck that was parked in the middle of the supermarket's parking lot. Someone had hung banners and bunting along the edge of the truck and it looked like a float in a parade. Up on the back they'd put chairs and a table and a lectern— a sort of podium where somebody might stand and give a speech. Doug had told me that Terry would talk but there might be a whole lot of other people who'd want to say a few things too.

As Terry walked along the length of the truck the dozen or so people up on the platform with him rose to their feet. They offered him their hands, or slapped him on the back or both. One of the women gave him a hug and then pulled him down so she could kiss him on the cheek. Terry sat down on a chair right beside the podium.

"He looks tired," Doug whispered in my ear.

"He must be. Running all day and then coming here."

Terry and Doug had checked into the motel, grabbed a meal and driven right over. My father had headed off someplace—he didn't say where—and I'd asked Doug if I could come along with them. I'd heard Terry speak before but I wanted to come anyway. After all, what was I going to do at the motel, watch TV?

"I feel bad," Doug said. "He needs to rest. But this whole run is about raising money and that's what these things do."

"There are a lot of people here," I said.

"That's a good thing. In the beginning of the run when Terry spoke there were times when there were only a few people, or a couple of dozen at the most."

"There have to be a few hundred people here," I said.

"There are over *four* hundred people here," Doug said.

"How do you know that?"

"That's how many there were when I stopped counting, and more people have come since then."

I looked around at the folks who surrounded us. There were families—mothers and fathers and small children and grandchildren all standing together. There were couples holding hands, people by themselves, groups of teenagers. They ranged in age from toddlers to seniors. There were at least two people in wheelchairs and lots of canes. Some of them were dressed in overalls and boots and looked like they'd come straight from the fields. A couple of men were in suits and ties. Most people were just in jeans and skirts and shirts. People were talking and smiling and laughing. There was a feeling like they were all going to a picnic, or waiting to get into a movie or a county fair.

"Good evening!" boomed out a voice. I turned to look at the stage as the voice echoed off the wall of the grocery store and back across the parking lot. There was a man standing at the podium.

"It's wonderful to see so many of my friends and neighbours here tonight," the man continued. "We're here to welcome a visitor to our town."

"Yea Terry!" a voice yelled from the crowd, and the whole audience started to clap and yell and yelp.

The man clapped along and then held his hands up to silence the crowd. It took a few more seconds for calm to be restored.

"I know none of you came out here to hear me speak—"

"That's for sure, Bob!" somebody called out, and a ripple of laughter rolled over the crowd.

"But since I'm your mayor I guess you're going to have to put up with a few of my words," he continued. "You all know the young man sitting here beside me."

The crowd broke into cheers and applause again. Terry gave a little smile and looked down at his feet.

"You know he's running across this country to raise money to find a cure for cancer. It's a brave thing he's doing. Something that makes me proud. I was born and raised in this town. There's hardly a person here tonight I haven't known all my life . . . just like there's hardly a person here who doesn't know me."

His voice cracked over the last few words like he was nervous.

"Three years ago in March my wife passed away . . . my wife of thirty years. She died of cancer. She fought hard. She didn't want to die, but in the end . . ." He reached a hand up to his face and brushed back tears that I couldn't see but could hear in his voice.

"Terry is running for my wife. And Bill Stevens's mother," he said, gesturing to somebody in the audience. "And Kathy McCurdy's grandfather," he said, pointing toward a woman up on the stage sitting right beside Terry. "And I could go on and on like that. There's nobody in this crowd, nobody in this town . . . heck, nobody in this country who hasn't been touched by cancer . . . hasn't lost somebody they loved." He wiped away more tears.

"I ask you now to put your hands together to welcome Terr—"

His words were lost as a wall of applause washed up and over the stage, and every single person on the back of the truck leapt to his feet. The mayor offered Terry his hand, and as they started to shake he pulled him forward and wrapped his arms around him.

Terry came to the podium and, unbelievably, the cheering got louder. He smiled and then looked down at the podium, like he was embarrassed. Slowly the applause began to fade to silence.

"Hi, I'm Terry," he began. "I hope you all can hear me. I'd like to start by telling you a little bit about me and why I'm running across Canada.

"I was eighteen and a first-year student in Kinesiology at Simon Fraser University in Vancouver, British Columbia. I played on the junior varsity basketball team. I had a pain develop on the right side of my knee for about a four- or five-month period. I didn't really think about it. I just figured I'd hurt something playing basketball. But it got worse and worse. One morning I woke up and it hurt so bad I couldn't even get up. I knew something was wrong, but I still thought I'd just done some damage, maybe ripped a cartilage or something." He paused. "They did some tests, and that day they told me that I had a malignant tumour and I'd have to have my leg taken off. Five days later my leg was amputated."

Terry paused again, and there was a complete hush over the audience. It felt like nobody even dared to breathe, like even the wind had stopped rustling in the trees.

"The night before the surgery my high school basketball coach, Terri Fleming, came to see me. He brought me an article about an amputee who ran in the New York Marathon. And I started to think, if he could do it, I could do it. I've always been competitive. I like challenges. I'm a dreamer. And that night I had a dream about running across Canada. That was when the Marathon of Hope really began.

"Right from the start it was a terrible shock, but I had encouragement and support from all kinds of people. So right from the beginning I took it as a challenge, and I thought about trying my best and showing everybody what could be done on one leg.

"I was lucky. I got cancer, but I survived. Today I feel privileged to even be alive. But as I think back to those first few months, how scared I was, not knowing whether I would live or die, I remember promising myself that should I live I would rise up to meet this new challenge face to face and prove myself worthy of life, something that people take for granted. Lots of other people who went through this with me weren't as fortunate. They died. And I remember those people. I remember their faces and the pain they went through. I couldn't just walk away and forget. I was determined to take myself to the limit. So after a year and a half of treatment and rehabilitation I decided to do something about that dream.

"I ran over three thousand miles in training. Then I knew it was time. And now I need your help," Terry continued. "If everybody could give just a dollar or two we can fight it . . . fight it together . . . try to defeat cancer. Somewhere the hurting must stop."

I felt a charge of electricity shoot right up my spine. I'd heard him say some of this same speech before, but it was like I was hearing each part for the first time. I couldn't believe the power of his words.

"I don't like to talk about it much, but sometimes I run in a lot of pain and I get tired . . . but I don't feel any pain when I get support like this. Thank you for taking the time to listen to me."

Everybody on the stage jumped to their feet, and the audience exploded—including both me and Doug. People clapped and screamed and cheered and hollered and whistled. There was a surge of people toward the truck and Terry. Doug took me by the arm and led me to the back, away from the crowd.

"That was amazing," I said.

"I've heard him speak a hundred times and it still gets to me," Doug said.

"I wish my father had been here," I said. "I have to tell him as soon as we get back."

"That could be a while," Doug said.

"Somebody else is going to make a speech?" I asked.

"I hope not. But it'll take a while anyway. People will want to shake Terry's hand, or tell him a story or ask him questions."

"And what do we do?"

"I don't know about you but I'm heading back to the van. If I'm lucky I can catch a few minutes of sleep. Four-thirty comes pretty early in the morning."

Chapter Sixteen

I CIRCLED AROUND the side of the motel. Our room was in the back. My father always liked his room away from traffic because he said the noise kept him awake. I dug into my pocket to find the key and—my father's rental car was parked in front of the room! He was back from wherever he'd been. I doubled my pace. I wanted to tell him all about what had happened tonight . . . the rally, the reaction of the people, the amount of money raised. They hadn't finished counting it all, but Doug figured there was about twelve thousand dollars!

I pushed in through the door. "Hello!" I yelled out.

He held up a hand to silence me—he was talking on the phone.

"Okay, sure, that sounds good," he said. "So I'll see you the day after tomorrow." He hung up the phone.

"Who was that?" I asked.

"My editor."

"He's coming out here?"

"No, we're going back to Toronto."

I guess I should have been glad to be going home, but I wasn't. "When do we leave?"

"We fly out of Moncton tomorrow evening, so we can even sleep in."

"What if I want to get up early and run with Terry?" I asked. "That is, if he wants me to run with him. Or I could just ride in the van. Could you come and get me? He's running toward Moncton anyway."

"I could do that . . . if you're sure that's what you want."

"I do, if it's okay with Terry."

"I thought you'd be more happy to be going home."

"I am . . . I guess," I said. I should have been happy. Instead I felt disappointed.

"I figured that being out here in the middle of nowhere wouldn't really be that exciting for you."

"Parts were exciting. You should have been there tonight. You should have heard Terry speak."

"Did he do well?"

"He did great! And there were hundreds and hundreds of people. I could tell you all about it and you could write a story and—"

"I really can't write about something I didn't witness. Besides, I've already written my story."

"You have?"

"Finished it about thirty minutes ago. It'll be in tomorrow's paper . . . and after that comes out maybe it's best that we aren't around any more."

"What do you mean?" I asked, although I had a terrible feeling I already knew.

"Terry may not like what I wrote. Copy's right there," he said, motioning to the desk. "Read it if you want."

I rushed over and grabbed the sheets of paper. I scanned down the page. It wasn't about the run, it was about Terry and Doug fighting, how Terry ordered Doug around and how there were days when the two of them hardly spoke to each other.

"You can't write this!" I snapped.

"Already did."

"But it shouldn't be in the papers. You shouldn't file this story."

"Too late. I phoned it in just before you got here."

"But you told me you'd let me read all the stories," I said.

"You weren't around. It's already been sent in."

"Then you have to phone them back and tell them not to run it!" I demanded.

He looked at his watch. "Even if I wanted to, it's probably too late. The presses start rolling right about now."

"So stop them!"

"If I did, there'd be a big gap in the paper. I don't have time to write another story, even if I did have an idea."

"You could write about the speech Terry gave tonight and how much money they raised—it's twelve thousand dollars, maybe even more, and—"

"I told you, I wasn't there so I can't write about it. Besides, I've found a different perspective."

"It may be different but it's wrong!"

"But it's *not* wrong," he said. "I've checked out my facts and everything I wrote is true."

"Whether it's true or not doesn't change the fact that it's wrong. You just shouldn't be writing about it."

"I'm a reporter. It's like I told you, I have an obligation to write the truth."

"Even if it hurts people?"

"I'm not trying to hurt people. I'm just writing a story." He paused. "Besides, you know I'm not making this up. You've spent a lot of time with them, you know that they fight."

I didn't say anything.

"Are you afraid they'll blame you for giving me the story?" he asked.

I kept my mouth clamped tightly shut, biting down on the inside of my mouth to stop myself from crying.

"I can't be the only one who's noticed," my father said. "The other reporters are bound to pick up on it sooner or later. I'm just the first out of the box with the story. If it hadn't been me it would have been somebody else."

"You should let it be somebody else! Just phone them up and kill the story!"

"I can't do that," he said. "It would mean missing a deadline, and I've never missed a deadline in my entire—"

I turned around, ran across the room, threw open the door and ran out.

"Winston!" my father called after me.

I ran along the back of the motel and disappeared around the corner. I kept running until I reached the edge of the woods and slipped into the trees. I didn't know if he was coming after me or not, but he wasn't going to find me. Not tonight. I didn't know where I was going, but I knew where I wouldn't be—in that room with him.

I pulled another quarter out of my pocket. Maybe this would have to be my last game. I only had twelve dollars in my pocket and I'd need most of that to eat. Especially since I'd decided I wasn't going back to the motel. There was no telling how long it would take to get to Toronto. I figured I'd just stick out my thumb and hitchhike back home. That could take a long time. Maybe days and days. It wasn't going to be as nice or fast or easy as taking a plane back with my father, but I didn't think I could stand to be around him right now, even for just the few hours I'd have to sit beside him in the plane.

How stupid could I be—asking him to kill that story. He didn't care about Terry. Why should he care about Terry when he didn't even care about me or my mother? Being a reporter, filing his stories was all that mattered to him . . . never missing his precious deadline. Sure, Dad, make sure you keep your commitment to the paper even if you don't keep your commitment to the people around you, the people you're supposed to take care of.

I went to put the quarter into the video game.

"So that's what a Frogger game looks like," said a familiar voice from over my shoulder.

I turned around and was shocked to see Terry standing right behind me. I practically jumped to the side. His hair was mussed up and he had his hands jammed into the pockets of one of his old warm-up jackets.

"What are you doing here?" I stammered.

"A better question is what are *you* doing here?"

I didn't know what to say. What did he know? "I'm just playing video games," I said, forcing out the words. Maybe he didn't even know that I'd taken off.

"I figured that part. I meant what are you doing here at eleven-thirty at night? Shouldn't you be sleeping?"Terry asked. He looked tired, and he shifted over so he could lean against the game.

"Me? What about you?" I asked. I always found it was better to answer a question with another question if you didn't want to answer the first question to begin with. "You really should be asleep."

"I was asleep. Sleeping soundly." He paused. "At least I was until your father came pounding on my door."

"He shouldn't have done that," I muttered. Had my father lost his mind, waking this guy up in the middle of the night?

Terry shrugged. "What choice did he have? He was pretty worried. Still is pretty worried, I imagine."

"There's nothing to worry about."

"That's what I told him, but you know how parents are. My parents still worry about me even though I'm not a kid any more."

"I'm not a kid either," I snarled.

"I never said you were. I tried to tell your father that too, but he had this strange idea that you were running away."

I felt a sudden rush of embarrassment. Just how much had my father told him, and how dare he tell people about what I'd done? My embarrassment was replaced by anger. Anger at my father . . . and anger at Terry. What was he doing here anyway, sticking his nose in where it didn't belong?

"I told him you probably just needed some time to cool off. I told him that I'm the same way when I get mad, and that you'd be back as soon as you were ready."

"If you think that, then why are you here?" I asked.

"Maybe I just wanted to play some Frogger. Somebody told me it was a really, really cool game."

"Yeah, right," I scoffed. But when I looked up I could see the hint of a smile on his face.

"Or maybe I came because I thought you might need a ride back to the motel. Doug is just outside in the van. We can drive you."

"If I want to get back I can just walk. I have *two* good legs, you know!"

I saw him flinch—I'd got to him . . . but I didn't feel good . . . I felt bad. That was such a stupid, hurtful thing to say.

"I guess I deserved that," Terry said. "I really came because I was worried. Worried that you were going to do the wrong thing."

"And just what do you think is the wrong thing?" I asked.

"Running."

I laughed. "And this coming from the guy running across Canada."

"There's a big difference. I'm not running *away* from anything." He paused. "Are you planning on running away?"

I didn't answer right away. "What will you do if I say yes?" I asked.

"I guess I'll try to convince you that you shouldn't."

"And if you can't convince me?" I asked.

"I'm hoping I can."

"But if you can't?"

He took a deep breath. "Then I'm going to have to stop you."

I looked past Terry and toward the door. The arcade wasn't big or wide but there was probably enough space for me to dodge by him and get out. Probably. Maybe.

"I know what you're thinking," Terry said. "Think you can make it?"

I didn't answer.

"Maybe you can. You're definitely quicker than I am. You proved that on the basketball court." He paused. "But you also have to figure that unless you're planning on running more than twenty-six miles tonight, *eventually* I'm going to catch you."

In spite of the seriousness of the situation I suddenly burst out laughing, and Terry smiled.

"And if you do decide to run and you manage to get by me to the door, I need you to do me a favour," he continued.

"What sort of favour?"

He nodded. "Could you at least run in that direction?" he said, pointing off to his left. "That's west. So if I do have to chase you at least we'll be heading in the right direction."

Terry flashed me a big smile and I couldn't help but smile back.

"How about if we drive you back instead?" he asked. "I'd really like that."

"I . . . I don't know if I can do it . . . I don't know if I can go back right now."

"Of course you can."

"It's hard . . . really hard."

"I know. But I also know you're the sort of person who can handle the hard stuff."

I shook my head. "I don't know."

"Believe me, I *do* know. I know you're no quitter. You can do whatever you want to do."

"You really think so?" I asked. I felt myself on the verge of tears.

He nodded. "How about if you and me make a deal?"

"What sort of deal?" I asked.

"You go back to the motel and then go back with your father to Toronto. You get home and you go to school—even though it's hard—and you *stay* at home."

"I don't want to make a promise I can't keep."

"You can keep it."

"You said there was a deal. What happens if I do those things?"

"Then I'll keep doing what I'm doing. One of us will run and the other one doesn't have to. What do you think?"

I let out a big sigh. I was fighting harder and harder not to cry.

"Well?" Terry asked.

"I can try."

"That's all I'm asking. There are no guarantees about anything in life. Lord knows I've learned that the hard way. I'm no quitter, and neither are you." Terry reached over and put a hand on my shoulder.

"Now it's time to go back to the motel. We both need some sleep so we can run tomorrow. Your father said you wanted to get up and run with me before you left. Are you still up for it?"

"Of course I am."

"Good. Oh, by the way, your father said that if I found you I should tell you something."

What did he want to tell me? My stomach tightened up.

"It didn't make much sense to me but he said you'd understand."

"What did he say?" I asked, though I was almost afraid to find out. Was he going to tell me how disappointed he was in me, how I'd let him down, how——?

"He said there's going to be a hole in tomorrow's paper because he missed his deadline."

"He said that?" I could hardly believe it.

"Maybe those weren't the exact words but that was the message. Do you understand what he meant?"

I nodded.

"Can you explain it to me?" Terry asked.

"I could . . . but I'm not going to. Can I get that drive now?"

"Sure. Although I was thinking that we could make Doug wait just a couple more minutes." Terry reached into his pocket and pulled out some quarters. "Since we're here anyway, could we play a couple of games of Frogger? I want to see what all the fuss is about."

Chapter Seventeen

"ARE YOU SURE you don't want to come with us?" I asked my mother.

"No, this is your time with your father and I'm not going to interfere with that. Especially when things are going so well."

In the six weeks since we'd come back from Nova Scotia my father and I had got together every week. Well, almost every week. He'd had to go on assignment in Europe for ten days so we'd met twice the week before he left.

"But I'd really like you to meet Terry," I said.

"I'd like that too, but not today. Maybe we can go out and meet him when he's running out of Toronto in a few days. He's going to be too busy to do much meeting with anybody today anyway."

I hadn't even thought of that. The TV and the papers had been reporting that it was going to be a massive rally and that he'd be surrounded by hundreds, maybe even thousands of people. Would he even have time to meet with me, to talk?

"Now you'd better get going. Get your shoes on and go downstairs and wait for your father." She looked at her watch. "He should be here soon . . . unless of course he's late, as usual. Some things don't change."

"But some things *do* change."

She gave me a little smile. "Yes, some things do change." She reached over and gave me a hug and a kiss on the cheek. "It wasn't that long ago that I had to bend down to give you a kiss and now I have to get up on my tippy-toes. You're growing up . . . in so many ways."

"I'm trying . . . as hard as I can."

"You're doing a lot more than trying." She gave me a kiss on the other cheek and then released me. "Just don't go rushing any of it. I'm in no hurry for you to grow all the way up."

"I'll take my time," I said.

"Good. Now you'd better get a move on if you want to get to Scarborough on time. The news report said they were expecting an incredible crowd."

"I definitely want to be there for the speech."

"I've heard he's quite an inspirational speaker," my mother said. "All I've heard are sound bites on the news. It would be different hearing him live, but I guess I'll have to settle for the radio. They're broadcasting his speech today on the CBC."

"That's so cool."

"Are you still planning on bringing your scrapbook?"

"I'm not sure," I said. I'd been collecting all the newspaper articles that had been written about the Marathon of Hope. The scrapbook was now fat and overflowing. I knew that before he got to Port Renfrew I'd need a second and third and maybe even a fourth scrapbook.

"Didn't you want him to autograph it?" my mother asked.

"I did, both Terry and Doug, but I don't know if I want to bother them. I'm not sure if I'll even be able to talk to Terry," I said. "He may not have time."

"Unless I misread those postcards he's sent you, he'll have time for you."

Terry had been sending me postcards every week or so from along the route. "He was just being polite. He's going to be awfully busy."

"I don't really know Terry, except for what you've told me and all the reports in the papers and on TV, but he strikes me as the sort of person who would never be too busy for his family or his friends. And you *are* one of his friends."

I smiled. "I guess I am."

"Good. I hear some people have been running along with him. Are you planning on running today?" she asked.

"I'm not really sure, but just in case I'm going to put on my running shoes, and I'm wearing a T-shirt and I have shorts on under my pants . . . so . . ."

"Excellent. And don't worry about the crowds and Terry being busy because, remember, you'll be with your father. You can count on his personality and his press pass to get you close enough to see Terry and have Terry see you. After all, your father is important . . . maybe not as important as he thinks he is but—"

"Mom . . ." I warned her. I'd told both my parents that I didn't want either of them ever saying anything bad about the other.

"All right, all right. I'm trying to be better too."

The buzzer sounded.

"Looks like your father is actually on time after all. It seems like *lots* of things can change."

"There's a parking spot!" I exclaimed.

My father hit the brakes and then eased us into the space.

"I can't believe how far away we're having to park," I said.

"I can't even see the Civic Centre from here," my father commented.

We got out of the car and joined a throng of people walking in the direction we wanted to go.

"This is going to be an incredible crowd," I said.

"The only thing bigger than the crowd is going to be our walk. I didn't think we'd be the ones walking halfway across Canada to get to this speech," my father said.

"Terry's not *walking* across Canada, he's *running*. Besides, I don't think a little exercise is going to hurt you," I said as I reached over and patted him on the belly.

"How about a little respect for your elders?"

"I always try to give you as little respect as possible," I joked. "Can we walk a bit faster? I'm afraid we won't be able to get in."

"Have no fear. We'll get in no matter how crowded it is. Remember, I'm the guy with the press credentials."

"That's right. Mom even said that they'd never keep somebody like you out, you know, somebody really important."

"She said that?" he asked. I could tell by the tone of his voice and his expression that he was both surprised and pleased.

I nodded. Of course I didn't say the part that she'd added to the end about him not being as important as he thought he was.

"Your mother is a pretty remarkable woman. Bright, beautiful and talented."

"Mom?"

"I guess the biggest mistake I ever made was letting her get away."

As I remembered it, he was the one that got away, or ran away. I didn't say that, though. One of the things I was learning was when to talk and when to shut up.

"No, that's wrong," my father continued. "That was the *second* biggest mistake I ever made."

"What was the biggest?" I asked, and then instantly regretted asking. Was he going to tell me that leaving his first wife was his biggest mistake?

"The biggest mistake I ever made was not spending enough time with my boys, both while I was married and afterwards. Marriages end, and a man and woman are no longer husband and wife. But fathers and sons are always fathers and sons. That should never change. That's one mistake I'm trying to fix. I *am* trying," he said.

"I know." I wanted to say something more, but words just wouldn't come out. But maybe I didn't need to say anything. I think he already knew.

We continued to move with and around the crowd. There had to be thousands and thousands of people, all of them moving toward the big building that I assumed was the Scarborough Civic Centre. Despite the crush of people, everybody was polite and friendly and smiling, and nobody was pushing or crowding against anybody else.

We came to the end of a line that was funnelling into one of the entrances to the building. My father moved along the side of the line and I trailed behind him. There were two uniformed policemen standing at the door and my father pulled out his wallet and showed them his I.D.—his press credentials. They waved him through and he grabbed me by the arm and towed me along behind him.

"One of the perks of being a reporter is that you get in to see the most important or interesting or scary things that are happening. Those officers don't even know if I'm covering this story or if I'm just here out of curiosity. Have you given any more thought to the idea of being a reporter?"

"I'm just working on having a good summer and a good start to grade nine in the fall." Actually, I'd mentioned it to my guidance counsellor at school and she'd said she thought that might be the job for me. I hadn't said anything about it to my parents yet, but I was going to, when I was more sure. I knew it would make them happy. Especially my father. It seemed only fair to want to make him happy now that he was trying to do the same with me.

The inside of the building was even more crowded than the outside. There were security guards directing the river of people up a set of stairs.

"Come this way," my father said, breaking out of the current of the crowd. He led me to an aisle. There were two more policemen guarding a door.

"Sorry, sir," one of the officers said, "but there's no more space on this level so you'll have to go upstairs."

"Press," my father said as he flashed his I.D. again.

The officer looked at it, and then my father, suspiciously. "It looks legitimate. Go on through," he said as he held the door open.

We entered. We were in a big chamber. It was even more packed than the lobby. I looked up at the big high ceiling that seemed to soar right up to the sky. There were levels and levels above the main floor—curving balconies—and people were hanging over the railings, packed together like sardines.

"This is where the Scarborough City Council meets," my father said. "The mayor would normally sit right over there."

In the centre of the room there was an open area, the only empty space in the place, and a podium. It was really just a fancier version of the back of that truck where I'd last seen and heard Terry speak. I guess the biggest difference was the half dozen microphones attached to the podium and the equal number of TV cameras that surrounded it. The thought of standing there at the very centre of all these people and all those cameras sent a shiver up my spine.

"Where are we going to sit?" I asked. It looked like, except for those few seats in the centre, every inch of floor space was already occupied.

"Stay with me."

My father wove his way through the crowd and I followed right behind. He led me to a little area over to the side. It was roped off and there was a sign that said "ACCREDITED PRESS" in big letters. He showed his I.D. a third time and we were admitted to that section. There were still some seats.

As we started to walk to those seats my father greeted and was greeted by other reporters. Some shook hands and a couple even threw their arms around him and gave my father a little hug. He seemed to know pretty well everybody, and they knew—and liked—him. My father made sure to introduce me to each one of them—"This is my boy, Winston . . . named after his old man"—and they were all friendly to me. We finally settled into two seats.

"This is quite the crowd, and I heard they're expecting at least five times as many people when he speaks at Toronto City Hall tomorrow."

"That's amazing," I said.

"It is." He paused. "The whole nation is watching Terry, following along with him as he runs across the country."

"It just keeps getting bigger and bigger," I said.

"I guess I was wrong," my father said.

"Wrong about what?"

"Remember when I said that the public was going to get tired of all of this . . . that they'd lose interest in this story?"

"Not really," I lied. I remembered that conversation very well. A couple of times over the past weeks I'd even thought about mentioning it to my father, but I hadn't. Why would I want to make him feel bad?

"You *must* remember. It was when we were in Nova Scotia and I was annoyed that I had to stay and keep covering the story. I said that it would only be news when he stopped running, and you disagreed. Don't you remember?"

"Sort of . . . maybe a little."

"And you said that it would get to be a bigger story with each day," my father said.

"Yeah, I guess a remember that a little bit."

"Well, one of us was right and one of us was wrong." He paused. "I just want you to know that even if you *really* don't remember the conversation, you had it figured out right and I didn't."

I didn't know what to say. I almost felt embarrassed. Embarrassed and proud. I *had* called it right.

"Is that your scrapbook?" he asked.

I nodded.

"Can I have a look?"

I handed him the book and he opened it up. "Here's the first article I wrote about Terry and the Marathon of Hope. That seems like such a long time ago."

"It's a very good article," I said.

"Thanks. Do you have any of the other stories I wrote?" he asked.

"I have all of your stories. Actually, I have all of the stories anybody has written in all three of the Toronto newspapers. Everything."

"That's impressive. Are there some articles that you like more than others?"

"There are a few that really didn't get it right," I said. "I don't like those ones. It makes me crazy when people question Terry's motives for the run, or suggest that he hasn't really run the whole way. I can just imagine how steamed Terry gets when he hears that!"

"And do you have a favourite article?" he asked.

"There's a lot I like . . . your first article is one of my favourites."

"*One* of your favourites? So which one do you like the very best?" he asked.

I took the book back from him and started to flip through the pages. "This one," I said, handing him back the book.

"This article by Christie Blatchford?"

I suddenly realized that maybe I shouldn't have done that—put a story by another reporter above one of his own. I didn't want to hurt his feelings. At least, I didn't want to do that any more.

"It's really my co-favourite . . . that one and the first one you wrote."

"I read this article when it came out," my father said. "It is one *great* story. And of all the words that have been written about Terry and the run, I think she has the very best. This line that says—"

"He gave us a dream as big as our country," I said, cutting him off.

"Exactly. I wish I had written that one. And believe me, that's the best compliment one reporter can give another reporter. That girl—I mean, that woman—can really write." He closed the scrapbook and handed it back to me. "You didn't just pick out a great article, you knew the line that made the article so good. You really do have what it takes to become a reporter . . . a *damn* fine reporter."

"Thanks," was all I could mumble. I felt a warm, melty feeling in my head.

"Would you like to meet Christie Blatchford? She's here somewhere."

"She is?"

My father stood up and craned his neck around. "I don't see her, but I know she's coming to cover the story. When I see her I'll introduce you. She'll get a real kick out of finding out that my own son thinks she's a better writer than me."

"I didn't say that!" I exclaimed. "I liked her story." I knew what I wanted to say next. I took a deep breath. "But my father is still the better reporter . . . the *best* reporter."

He smiled. A big smile. "That's nice of you to say, even if you don't really be—"

Suddenly his words were lost in a swell of noise. People started to clap and cheer and everybody rose to their feet, blocking my view. I jumped up and saw Terry walking up the aisle and toward the podium.

Chapter Eighteen

THE NOISE GOT LOUDER and louder and louder as Terry approached the centre, until it felt like the whole building was actually shaking. He was followed by a whole procession of people. His face was tanned and his hair was longer than before—sort of wild looking and tangled—and though he had a big smile he looked kind of tired. He was dressed to run, wearing his Marathon of Hope T-shirt, shorts and running shoes. In his hand he held a small yellow flower—a daffodil.

"Do you know who those people are?" my father asked.

"I recognize his brother Darrell from the pictures in the papers and on TV," I said. Darrell had joined Doug and Terry on the Marathon about five weeks before. I'd been thinking how it would be nice for everybody to have him along. I knew how much Terry had been missing his family. And—who knew?—maybe Darrell had been emptying the toilet's holding tank occasionally.

"I'll tell you something that even Terry doesn't know," my father said.

"What?"

"I just heard about it in the newsroom before I picked you up."

"What? What did you hear?"

"You have to promise to keep it to yourself."

"Of course I will!"

My father smiled. "His whole family was flown out from British Columbia to surprise him. He'll be meeting them later on today."

"Terry is going to be thrilled!" I exclaimed.

"I'm sure he will be," my father agreed. "I'm actually trying to arrange an interview with his parents while they're in town. I want to see what sort of people they are, although I think I already know."

"You do?" I asked.

"Sure. The fruit doesn't fall far from the tree. I bet you they're honest, hardworking, determined and more than a little bit stubborn."

"Like Terry."

"Like Terry," he said. "Do you see Doug anywhere?"

"No, but he's got to be here somewhere . . . probably making a phone call and planning what comes next. I don't think he ever stops."

A woman walked over to the podium. There was a sign on it that I hadn't noticed before. In big letters it said "Scarborough Welcomes Terry Fox and The Marathon of Hope." The woman tapped on the microphone and the sound echoed throughout the cavernous chamber. The crowd noise faded away.

She cleared her throat. "Thank you, ladies and gentlemen and boys and girls, for welcoming, with me, this courageous, determined young man who has come to Scarborough today to bring his message to us."

The crowd started to cheer and Terry took a step toward the podium. The woman gave him a hug, then stepped away and joined in the applause that was raining down on him. Terry's smile got wider, but he looked embarrassed. He looked down at the little flower. He twirled it in his hand as he waited for the applause to fade.

"I'm overwhelmed," Terry began. "This is unreal." He paused and looked up at the curving, swirling balconies that surrounded and rose above him. The expression on his face reflected the words he'd just spoken, as though he couldn't believe that all these people had come to hear him speak. I thought back to what Doug had told me about how when he'd first started there were sometimes only a few people present. And I couldn't help thinking about what it would be like—how big the crowd would be—when he finally reached the Pacific Ocean.

"I think you've all heard my story," Terry began, and the crowd erupted into laughter, cheers and applause.

"This all began with a pain in my leg. I didn't think it was anything, just something that I'd hurt playing sports. Instead they told me I had cancer, a type of cancer called an osteogenic sarcoma—bone cancer. To save my life they had to take off my leg. That night, waiting for the surgery, I had the idea about running to raise money for cancer research. I've always been competitive, and I wanted to show myself, and other people, too, that I could do it. To show them that I wasn't disabled or handicapped. My run is about ability and not disability. I wanted them to know that I was a survivor of cancer and not a victim. Nobody is ever going to call me a quitter."

"You tell 'em, Terry!" somebody shouted from the audience, and people began cheering wildly. Terry's smile grew and he looked down at the little yellow flower again. The crowd quieted down, wanting to hear him speak.

"Knowing that there are people like all of you who care about what I'm doing, that I'm not just running across Canada, that there are people who are giving money to help fight the disease that took my leg and to help other people who are lying down in hospital beds all over the world—that means so much to me. It's a great reward for me, the responses of the people and the way you've accepted what I'm doing. Thank you for coming here . . . for so many of you coming out to support the Marathon of Hope and to help raise money for cancer research."

Again the audience erupted in applause.

"One thing hurts me, though. People keep saying 'Terry Fox.' I'm not doing the run to become rich or famous. One of the problems with our world is that people are getting greedy and selfish. I'm not getting a cent of the money raised. It's all going where it belongs . . . to cure cancer." He paused and took a deep breath. It was so quiet you could hear a pin drop. "To me, being famous myself is not the idea of the run, and it wasn't the idea from the very beginning. To me, the only important part about the publicity is that cancer can be beaten, and the Marathon of Hope. And I'm just one member of the Marathon of Hope. I'm no different from anybody else. I'm no better, I'm no lower, I'm equal with all of you, and if I ever change that attitude myself then there's no point in continuing. So when you're . . . um . . . when you're . . . cheering and clapping for me, you're not just cheering and clapping for me."

His voice broke and I knew he was on the verge of tears.

"There's so many other people involved in the run that . . . that nobody hears about. There's my brother Darrell, and Doug and . . ."

The crowd started to clap and cheer and Terry waited for the reaction to fade.

"Bill Vigars raises money for cancer . . . he . . . ah . . . you see, I'm trying my very best . . . I run as hard as I can all day and I do my best, and sometimes we have to change the schedule, and whenever we have to do that he has to tell people ahead of time, and he gets all the hassles, and I don't think it's fair. Anybody who complains about any change in schedule, come up to me and tell me I'm not trying hard enough."

There was a groan of disbelief from the audience—how could anybody ever think that?—and then everybody started clapping and cheering again.

"Everybody who is here—everybody who gives even a dollar—is part of the Marathon of Hope and is helping us. . . . Sometimes I get tired." He paused. "And when I'm tired I think of the people who had cancer and just remember that I'm setting an example for other people and keep going to do my best." He paused again. "And even if I don't finish . . ."

What did he mean, even if he didn't finish? Of course he was going to finish . . . he was unstoppable . . . of course he was going to finish!

" . . . we need people to continue. It's got to keep going without me. It has to keep going . . . no matter what.

Somewhere the hurting must stop . . . and maybe that place is here. Thank you."

The whole crowd began clapping and cheering and screaming, but instead of the applause dying down it just got louder and louder and louder until it felt as if the building wasn't just shaking, it felt like it might collapse!

Terry walked down the aisle and people reached out to touch him or shake his hand. Everybody was on their feet cheering, waving flags, yelling, laughing and crying. Lots of people were crying.

"If we're going to talk to him we'd better get going," my father said. We left our seats and began weaving through Terry's supporters. The density of the crowd was incredible, and it was difficult to inch our way along.

"Winston!"

I turned around, trying to pick the voice out of the crowd. Who was calling me?

"Winston!"

It was Doug! We moved through the crowd in his direction as he made his way toward us. Doug shook hands with both me and my father.

"It's good to see you," he said.

"It's *great* to see you. How are things going?" I asked.

"Really good . . . hectic and tiring . . . but really good . . . really unbelievable." He gestured around the cavernous chamber. "I can't believe all of this."

"It is quite the crowd," my father agreed, "although I've heard that the rally at the Toronto City Hall tomorrow is going to be a lot bigger than this."

"Bigger than this?" Doug asked, as though he couldn't quite

understand how that could be possible.

"I think they're predicting somewhere around ten thousand people at Nathan Phillips Square. And of course that doesn't include all those people who are going to line the run route between here and there. I overheard two policemen talking about how people are already standing and waiting on the roads to see the rest of the run today."

"Amazing," Doug said, shaking his head.

"I thought you'd be pretty used to the crowds by now," my father said.

"I don't think I'll ever get used to crowds, and they just keep getting bigger and bigger," Doug said. "It's really good, though. I mean, more people means more donations and more money raised for cancer research. Besides, everybody is so friendly."

"Why wouldn't they be friendly?" I asked. "You and Terry are heroes."

"I'm no hero."

"Weren't you listening to Terry's speech?" I asked.

"I heard it. That doesn't mean I agree with everything he says all the time." Doug looked at his watch. "Time to go."

"I know it's pretty crazy today, but do you think that Winston could say hello to Terry before you leave?" my father asked.

Doug looked confused. "Say hello? Aren't you going to be running with us today?"

"Can I?" I exclaimed.

"Terry told me to keep an eye out for you."

"How did you even know I was here?"

"Just figured. You promised us you'd see us in Toronto, and we knew you'd keep your word. So, you're welcome to join us . . .

if you think you can keep up. As long as that's all right with your dad. . . ?"

"It's more than just all right," my father answered.

"Can I join you in the van if I get tired . . . maybe listen to a little Johnny Cash?" I asked with a grin.

Doug laughed. "I'm not driving the van today."

"You're not?"

"A volunteer is driving. I'm going to be running as well. So is Terry's brother Darrell, so you'll get to meet him."

"I'd like that."

"I'll take your scrapbook," my father offered.

I handed it to him. "Where should I meet you?" I asked.

"We're going to be stopping at the Four Seasons Hotel on Avenue Road. Your dad could wait for us there," Doug suggested.

"Isn't that a long way from here?"

"About twelve miles," Doug answered.

"Twelve miles!" I exclaimed. "I don't know if I can run that far!"

"You can," Doug said quietly.

That was an awfully long way to run. I'd never run twelve miles in my entire life.

"I'll be right there with you the whole way. If you get tired I'll drop back with you," Doug said.

"I could pick you up partway," my father offered.

"He could," Doug agreed, "but I *know* you can go the distance."

I looked at my father. "I'll see you at the hotel."

"Excellent." Doug turned to me. "It's pretty hot running on the asphalt. You have the right shoes . . . too bad you don't have shorts."

"I do! I'm wearing them underneath. I'll just slip off my pants."

I undid my belt and the button, pulled down the fly and began to pull my pants off. I struggled as they got caught and tangled around my running shoes. People were trying to get around us and I was taking up a lot of space. Maybe this wasn't the smartest way to do it. I lifted up one leg and pulled harder, teetering and almost falling over. My father reached over to steady me. I just couldn't get the pants off! I felt like such an idiot!

"Maybe if you pulled them back up you could take off your shoes," my father suggested. I could tell that he and Doug were working hard not to laugh—I appreciated that.

"No, they're coming . . . if I just pull a little harder—" There was a loud ripping sound and my foot popped free. I didn't even want to look at what I'd done to my pants, but really, I didn't care. I struggled with the second leg and I felt my shoe slip off and then it and my foot came free. I tossed the inside-out, torn and crumpled pants to my father, then bent down and quickly put the shoe back on.

"There, I'm ready to go!" I said, jumping to my feet.

"Not quite," Doug said.

"What do you mean?"

He hesitated. "After seeing you change into your shorts maybe this isn't such a good idea . . . but here . . . this is for you."

Doug handed me a T-shirt. I took it from his hands and looked at it. On the front it said "Terry Fox, Marathon of Hope." It was just like the T-shirts Terry and Doug always wore.

"This is for me?"

"Of course. Weren't *you* listening to Terry's speech? You're part of the Marathon of Hope too. Terry wanted you to have it."

"Should I put it on?" I asked, still feeling honoured and overwhelmed.

He nodded. "But I have one suggestion."

"You do?"

"After seeing you get down to your shorts, I think that maybe you should just *slip* it on over top of the shirt you're already wearing."

Doug led me through the crush of people and out the big double doors. Now that we'd left the building the crowd was more spread out but, still, there wasn't any place that wasn't filled with somebody.

"Feeling nervous?" Doug asked.

"A little bit," I admitted.

"About the distance you're going to run or about the size of the crowd?"

"Both."

"The run is simple. Don't think of it as twelve miles," Doug said. "Just take it one step at a time . . . one corner at a time . . . one mile at a time. That's the way Terry does it."

"And the crowd?" I asked.

"That you never get used to. I can't get over how Terry handles it so well. You know me, usually I just kind of blend into the background. But Terry, he's always the very centre of it . . . every eye is always on him, watching his every step, or misstep, listening to his every word. It's been hard. Maybe harder than the running itself."

"Is that why Terry looks so tired?" I asked.

"He runs all day and gives speeches every evening. Everybody wants to talk to him, spend time with him. He's wearing down."

"Maybe he should stop and take a rest."

Doug smiled. "I think we've had this conversation . . . and believe me, Terry and I have talked about it, but it can't happen . . . not now . . . not until it's over."

We stopped at the edge of a huge crowd. I caught sight of Terry in the very middle. He was surrounded by police officers.

"You know," Doug said, "in so many ways he's the same person I knew in grade eight—the same Terry. Then in other ways he's so different. It's like he's grown up before my eyes over the past three months . . . he's become . . . so much *more*."

Doug slipped through the crowd and I followed behind. Terry saw me and his face broke into a big smile, but he kept on talking to people and signing autographs for the police officers. We stopped just off to his side.

He handed back a piece of paper to one of the officers. "Winston!" he called out. He rushed forward and threw his arms around me, giving me a big hug. "It's great to see you!"

"It's great to see you, too!"

"Nice T-shirt."

"I really like it."

"I thought you would," he said. "I'd like you to meet somebody. This is my brother—"

"Darrell," I said, completing his sentence.

"Hi," Darrell said, extending a hand. We shook. "Good to meet you."

"Good to meet you . . . I've been reading a lot about you."

"That's a little scary. Terry told me all about *you*, too," Darrell said.

I wondered how much he had told him, and I was hoping he'd

left some of the bad stuff out. I felt embarrassed thinking about some of the things I'd said and done.

"Terry said you'd probably be joining us today. Are you ready to run?" Darrell asked.

"I'm ready."

"Good, because it's almost time to go," Doug said, checking his watch again. "We still have a schedule to keep."

"Do we have a minute before we have to go?" Terry asked.

"A minute or two," Doug answered.

"Good . . . I was hoping to talk to Winston."

"Sure, no problem," Doug said. "We'll hang on a bit."

Doug and Darrell walked away, leaving Terry and me alone—alone, that is, if you didn't count the hundreds of people who surrounded us.

"So, how have you been doing?" Terry asked.

"Fine. I've been doing fine."

"School?"

"I went to school every day."

"And your marks?" he asked.

"Not great, but good enough to pass. I'm going into grade nine next year, high school."

"High school was one of my favourite times. You're going to love it . . . you know, maybe trying out for some teams . . . going to classes every day . . . getting good marks."

"I'm going to do all of those things," I said. "A deal is a deal."

Terry flashed a big smile. "And home?"

"I'm there every day and every night. Like I said, a deal is a deal."

"That's what I wanted to hear . . . what I *knew* I'd hear. I knew you'd keep your word," Terry said.

"What choice did I have?" I asked. "You kept yours."

"I'm trying. I got this far and I'm not quitting . . . and neither can you. Agreed?"

"I'll keep my word. You can do the running for both of us."

"Except today you're going to be doing a little running too, right?"

"I'll be running."

"All right. It's really good to have you with us again," Terry said.

"It's good to be here, but this is all pretty overwhelming," I said.

"I've been doing this day by day and it still keeps on amazing me. It keeps getting bigger and bigger."

"But that's okay, isn't it?" I asked.

"More people, more money raised. But more time spent talking to people and going to rallies . . . that stuff gets to be more exhausting than the running."

"You looked tired," I said.

"I am, but you know," Terry said, "there's not another thing in the entire world I'd rather be doing."

I smiled. "Really?"

"Really."

Doug walked over. "It's time."

"You're going to take care of Winston?" Terry asked.

"He'll be running right beside me and Darrell the whole way."

That sounded good to me. I wasn't going to let Doug out of my sight for a second.

"Great. I'll see you in a while."

Terry turned and walked away, policemen on all sides to shepherd him through the crowd. I stayed close to Doug and

Darrell as they followed behind. Terry came to the very edge of the crowd. There were four more policemen on motorcycles waiting on the street, their machines rumbling away. They started slowly down the road, their lights flashing. The road was empty, but the sidewalks on both sides of the street were packed with people. Terry started running, and a wave of applause rose up from the crowd. I stood there, transfixed, watching him run. Stride, skip, step. Stride, skip, step. That same run that I'd witnessed in Nova Scotia. That same run that had taken him from St. John's, Newfoundland, all the way to Toronto. That same relentless pace that had now taken him over two thousand miles.

"It's time for us to run," Doug said. "Let's go."

Doug and Darrell and I started to run. As we pulled away from the crowd, a wall of runners started up behind us. We were a few dozen yards behind Terry. From that vantage I took in the whole scene—packed sidewalks, the clapping, yelling, signs waving—Terry the very centre of everything, just as Doug had said. People kept jumping out of the crowd and running along with us for a while before dropping back or stopping. There were men in suits, women who hiked up their skirts, little kids with their parents, people with their dogs, women in curlers and aprons who looked like they'd run straight out of the beauty salon as Terry passed and couldn't help joining in. There were volunteers holding buckets and bags, and people continually stuffed money into those containers. I couldn't even imagine just how much money was being raised.

As Terry ran he smiled and laughed, and for what had to be the seven millionth time, waved back at somebody. And I knew that what he had told me was right—there was no place else he would have rather been. There was nothing else he would rather have been doing.

And I also knew there was no place else I would rather have been. I was there watching, witnessing, being a part of something so much bigger than anything I could imagine . . . something that hadn't just started two thousand miles ago in Newfoundland and wasn't going to end in Port Renfrew . . . something bigger . . . so much bigger. Even bigger than the width of this whole country.

Chapter Nineteen

THE INTERCOM BUZZER SOUNDED and I clicked off the TV, got up off the couch and walked over to the door. I wondered who it could be. The buzzer sounded again. Whoever it was, they were in a hurry. I pressed the button to speak.

"Hello?"

"Hi, Winston, it's me."

"Dad?"

"Yeah, let me in."

"Sure." I pressed the button that opened the door to the lobby.

What was my father doing here in the middle of the day, and without calling? And why was he coming upstairs? He never came up here. He hadn't been in the apartment since he'd left, almost two years ago. My parents had been getting along better the past while, but he still always picked me up and dropped me off in the lobby.

A chill went up my spine. Whatever the reason for this, it couldn't be good. *Come on, don't be so paranoid . . . it doesn't necessarily mean anything,* I said to myself.

There was a knock. I opened up the door, and I could tell by his expression that something was wrong, terribly wrong . . . but what? I got an awful, sick feeling in the pit of my stomach.

My father came into the apartment. "I'm so glad you're—"

"Is Mom okay?" I demanded, cutting him off.

"Your mother? Of course she's okay."

I exhaled deeply. Thank goodness.

"I just spoke to your mother a few minutes ago. She's coming right home," my father said.

"Why is she leaving work early? And why are *you* here?"

He didn't answer right away. "You haven't heard, have you?"

"Heard what?" I demanded.

"It's Terry."

"Terry . . . what happened to Terry?" Now I was scared in a different way. I could feel my stomach tighten into a knot.

"He's stopped running."

I shook my head. "That can't be right. Terry would never stop running . . . that's *impossible*."

"I'm sorry to be telling you this, but I know how much he means to you, and I thought it would be best if you heard it from me or your mom."

"You're wrong!" I snapped. "He hasn't stopped! He wouldn't stop!"

"I wish I were wrong. I just heard the first reports coming into the newsroom. He had to stop."

"You mean for a couple of days, right?"

"I don't know all the details. When I spoke to your mother she said they were going to be doing news updates on the CBC."

I wanted to rush over and turn on the TV, but it felt like my feet were glued to the ground, like my legs were filled with lead. I just couldn't move.

"Winston?" my father asked. "Are you okay?"

I looked up at my father. He looked scared, which made me feel even worse. He reached over and took my arm and led me down the hall toward the living room. Suddenly I no longer felt heavy. Instead I felt like a balloon, being pulled along by my father. He grabbed the converter and clicked it on. It was showing the cartoon I'd been watching when I'd buzzed him up to the apartment. He clicked the channel, then clicked it again, and again and—and there was Terry. He was on a stretcher being loaded into the back of an ambulance!

I felt my legs get weak and I slumped down into a chair.

Terry looked so weak, so fragile.

"This footage was shot this afternoon outside of Thunder Bay," an unseen announcer said, "as Terry Fox was forced to abandon his run."

I heard the words and saw the images but I couldn't believe them, couldn't understand what they meant. It was as if the announcer were speaking in an entirely different language.

"Our correspondent at the scene reports that Terry was weak and fatigued."

"Of course he's weak and fatigued, you idiot!" I screamed at the TV. "Wouldn't you be tired if you'd run more than three thousand miles!" I turned to my father. "He just needs a rest . . .

he's been needing a rest for a long time. Just a few days off and then he'll be fine . . . he'll start running again!"

"Terry began his run this morning but had to abandon his efforts after twenty miles because he had difficulty breathing," the announcer continued. "Preliminary, and still unconfirmed reports indicate that our greatest fears have perhaps become true—that the primary cancer that cost Terry his leg has now spread. It appears that after 143 days and 3,339 miles the Marathon of Hope may have finally come to an end."

"You're wrong!" I screamed. "You're wrong!" I leaped off the chair, charged across the room and smashed the off button with the palm of my hand! The whole wall unit holding the TV shook and rocked and for a split second I thought it was going to come tumbling down on top of me!

"Winston!"

I spun around. "He's wrong! He doesn't know Terry. He wouldn't stop. He couldn't stop!"

"I'm so sorry."

"Are you?" I demanded. "You said it would only be a story when he stopped running!" Instantly I regretted my words. What an awful thing to say!

"I'm so sorry," my father repeated. "Sorry for you . . . sorry for Terry . . . sorry for the whole country . . . just plain sorry."

My lower lip started to quiver and I felt my tongue getting big and fat and the tears starting up, and I tried to fight it but I couldn't. I started to cry—big hard sobs from the pit of my stomach. The tears just flowed down my face, and my father threw his arms around me and held on as the sobs just kept coming and coming and coming and my whole body convulsed.

And then I felt another pair of arms around me and I looked up to see my mother—I hadn't heard her come in, but it was so good to have her arms around me too, holding on tight . . . holding me tight. It felt like I was little and my parents were together again, and I'd fallen down and hurt myself and they were both there to help make things better. Except this time, nobody could make things better. Nobody. This couldn't be happening, it couldn't. It wasn't fair. It just wasn't fair.

Chapter Twenty

AS I CAME IN THE DOOR I heard the phone ringing. I dropped my backpack and books fell out and slid across the floor. I rushed over and grabbed the phone off the table.

"Hello?"

"Hi, Winston."

I could hardly believe it. "Terry!"

"I was hoping I'd catch you," he said. "Although I thought you might still be at school."

"I just got in the door."

"How did it go?"

"Better than I thought it might . . . I was worried."

"Worried about what?" Terry asked.

"First day in high school," I said. "You know, it's so much bigger, so many more kids, the halls are crowded and everything."

"High school is a big step, but I know you can handle it. I wanted to call you," he said. "I guess you've heard about everything."

Of course I'd heard. The whole country knew that he'd had to stop running and that the cancer had returned. What was I supposed to say to him? "Um . . . um . . . how are you doing?" I finally managed to croak.

"I've been better."

"I've been watching the television reports, reading the papers," I said, still hoping that somehow all those reports were wrong.

"The cancer that was in my leg has gone to my lungs." Terry spoke softly, his voice cracking over the last few words.

"Terry . . . I'm so sorry."

"I wanted you to understand that I had no choice. I had to stop running. I had to go home," he said, his voice barely audible. "I had to have some more tests and X-rays, and maybe they're going to have to do an operation that will involve opening up my chest. Or it could be more drugs."

I started to cry. "It's just not fair," I blurted out. "It just shouldn't be happening to you."

"You know, you're the second person who's said that to me."

"Who was the first?"

"My father. Although he wasn't really saying it to me. He thought I was sleeping and he was talking to my mother. It was when we were flying home. And I'm going to say to you the same thing I said to him." There was a pause. "It's not fair or unfair . . . why *not* me?" Terry asked. "Why *shouldn't* it be happening to me?"

I started crying louder.

"It's going to be okay, Winston. This is just a setback. I'm not giving up," Terry said. "Right now I'm going to fight as hard as I can to beat cancer . . . as hard as I've fought to run across the country."

I wanted to say something, but I didn't know what, and even if I had been able to think of the words, I didn't think I could have forced them to come out.

"Winston, I need you to know that I had to stop running right now, but I haven't quit. And I need you not to quit either."

"Me?" I whispered.

"We made a deal, and you have to keep up your end. Keep going to school. Keep trying. Because you have to know that if there's any way I can get back out there and finish it, I will." I heard Terry take a big breath, and I could tell he was working hard not to cry. "Good things and bad things happen in the world, and I'm somebody who's going to try his hardest." There was a long pause. "And Winston, even if I die of cancer . . . even if I die . . . I want you to know that my spirit didn't die and that I kept on trying . . . that I never gave up."

"I know . . . And neither will I, Terry . . . neither will I."

After Note

TERRY BATTLED VALIANTLY for ten months. On June 28, 1981, he died at the Royal Columbian Hospital in New Westminster, British Columbia. He was one month short of his twenty-third birthday, and his family was at his side.

As Terry had foretold, his spirit did not die. He lives on through the work of the Terry Fox Foundation and the efforts of millions of people around the world who support cancer research in his name.

The Terry Fox Foundation strives to keep alive the heroic effort and integrity that Terry Fox embodied, while recognizing the duality of its mandate. Not only does it raise money for research, but it also continues to share Terry's story. People from around the world learn about Terry in the hope that their lives might be enriched by his example and that they may derive inspiration from his courage.

The Terry Fox Foundation raises funds for cancer research primarily through the annual Terry Fox Run. It is a grassroots organization that does not allow any commercialization of the Run, nor does it allow individuals or organizations to use the Terry Fox name or his likeness for personal gain. Please contact the Terry Fox Foundation to offer your support or to learn more about Terry Fox:

Toll free:	1-888-836-9786
Email:	national@terryfoxrun.org
Website:	www.terryfoxrun.org

Author's Note

A FEW YEARS AGO I was in Ottawa with my family when, across from Parliament Hill, I unexpectedly came upon a statue of Terry Fox. I stood beside that statue, unable to take my eyes from it. Overwhelmed by an incredible rush of memories and emotions, I sat down on a little bench just off to the side and stared. I thought about how many years had passed, but how the memories remained so strong—how an entire country was transfixed and united in Terry's quest—how he remains the most significant hero in my lifetime. I sat there, thinking, feeling, and brushed back the tears that came.

Then, the teacher and writer in me began wondering: why has there never been a novel written for young people about Terry? I knew that through the Terry Fox Foundation and the annual run in schools across the country his memory and goals have been kept alive for children. But what did these students really know about Terry, the person, and the details of the

Marathon of Hope? I decided right there, beside Terry, that I wanted to write that novel.

My first step was to approach the Terry Fox Foundation and the Fox family. I made it clear from the outset that I would write this novel only with the full agreement of the family. And I understood their initial caution—they are the guardians of Terry's name, legacy and dream.

Terry himself had previously given permission for a book to be written: *Terry Fox, His Story*. This wonderful work, written by Leslie Scrivener, is the authorized biography. Published in 1981 and revised in 2000, it is a factual account of Terry's life, his journey through the Marathon of Hope and the continuation of his legacy through the work of the Terry Fox Foundation.

That book was based completely on the facts. My book, a novel, is a blend of fact and fiction. The characters of Winston and his parents are fictional creations. I hope that through these characters the reader will be able to feel as though he or she has met Terry and shared the journey that was the Marathon of Hope.

In crafting my story I have tried, as much as possible, to take Terry's words directly from his speeches, writings and the videos recording the Marathon. In many places, however, I have had to craft dialogue—try to think what Terry or Doug might have said. It was incredibly reassuring to have the family provide feedback, and Terry's brother Darrell, who was a part of the Marathon and is now national director of the Terry Fox Foundation, was especially helpful in this way.

There are two places where I have changed the time frame of events to emphasize part of the true story. The episode Doug describes in which they couldn't find the marker and Terry ran an additional three miles to make sure he had covered the entire route actually took place two weeks after it does in my story. As well, the headline by Christie Blatchford, "He gave us a dream as big as our country," was written after Terry had been forced to stop running, and not prior to his speech at the Scarborough Civic Centre. I felt that this was perhaps the best, most descriptive, most powerful line ever written about the Marathon of Hope, and I wanted to include it.

Through my research and my contact with the Fox family and Doug Alward, I have come to an even greater appreciation of Terry and his accomplishments. He was a hero—a man of incredible strength and determination whose legacy and spirit live on through his family and the work of the Foundation.

All of my royalties, along with a contribution from the publisher, go directly to the Terry Fox Foundation. I am honoured to have been able to write Terry's story, and to have helped, in a small way, to raise funds for ongoing research to find a cure for cancer.

Eric Walters
Toronto, August 2003

Terry's Letter Requesting Support for His Run

The night before my amputation, my former basketball coach brought me a magazine with an article on an amputee who ran in the New York Marathon. It was then I decided to meet this new challenge head on and not only overcome my disability, but conquer it in such a way that I could never look back and say it disabled me.

But I soon realized that that would only be half my quest, for as I went through the 16 months of the physically and emotionally draining ordeal of chemotherapy, I was rudely awakened by the feelings that surrounded and coursed through the cancer clinic. There were faces with the brave smiles, and the ones who had given up smiling. There were feelings of hopeful denial, and the feelings of despair. My quest would not be a selfish one. I could not leave knowing these faces and feelings would still exist, even though I would be set free from mine. Somewhere the hurting must stop . . . and I was determined to take myself to the limit for this cause.

From the beginning the going was extremely difficult, and I was facing chronic ailments foreign to runners with two legs in addition to the common physical strains felt by all dedicated athletes.

But these problems are now behind me, as I have either out-persisted or learned to deal with them. I feel strong not only physically, but more important, emotionally. Soon I will be adding one full mile a week, and coupled with weight training I have been doing, by next April I will be ready to achieve something that for me was once only a distant dream reserved for the world of miracles—to run across Canada to raise money for the fight against cancer.

The running I can do, even if I have to crawl every last mile.

We need your help. The people in cancer clinics all over the world need people who believe in miracles.

I am not a dreamer, and I am not saying that this will initiate any kind of definitive answer or cure to cancer. But I believe in miracles. I have to.

Terry Fox
October 1979

Terry's Journey

Terry's Marathon of Hope started on April 12, 1980, in St. John's, Newfoundland, and ended just outside Thunder Bay, Ontario, on September 1, 1980. He ran 5,373 kilometres in 143 days.

This is the diary of Terry's journey, much of it excerpts from the journal he wrote in along the way:

April 12: 0 km   **St. John's, NF**
Terry Fox dips his artificial leg into the Atlantic Ocean and sets out on his Marathon of Hope.

April 21: 346 km   **Gander, NF**
"It was an exciting day in Gambo. People came and lined up and gave me ten, twenty bucks just like that. And that's when I knew that the Run had unlimited potential."

April 26: 542 km   **South Brook Junction, NF**

"Today we got up at 4:00 a.m. As usual, it was tough. If I died, I would die happy because I was doing what I wanted to do. How many people could say that? I went out and did fifteen push-ups in the road and took off. I want to set an example that will never be forgotten."

May 6: 882 km   **Port-aux-Basques, NF**

Port-aux-Basques, population 10,000. Raises $10,000, equal to one dollar per person. Several weeks after Terry left Newfoundland, he finds out that this total increased by another $4,000.

May 13: 1,234 km   **Highway 7, NS**

"Twenty-six miles is now my daily minimum. It is beautiful, quiet, peaceful country. I love it."

May 15: 1,278 km   **Sheet Harbour, NS**

After a reception where Terry ran with some schoolchildren, he writes, "When I ran with the kids I really burned it just to show them how fast I could go. They were tired and puffing. All right!"

May 20: 1,373 km   **Dartmouth, NS**

"I ran to the vocational school here with fifty students. I ran about a mile. They had raised about $3,000. What a great group of kids! Too bad not everybody was doing that."

May 26: 1,728 km   **Charlottetown, PEI**

"There were lots of people out to cheer me on and support me. Incredible! . . . I had another dizzy spell during the Run. Still

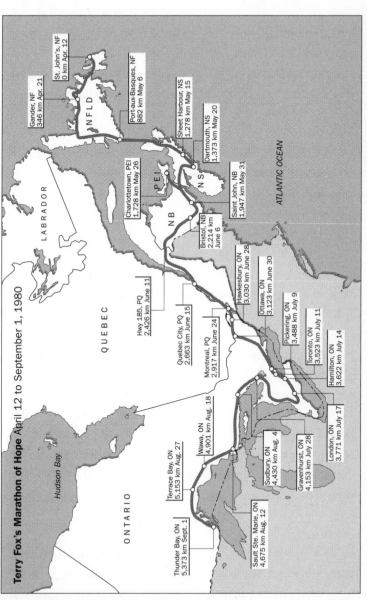

Terry Fox's Marathon of Hope April 12 to September 1, 1980

St. John's, NF
0 km Apr. 12

Gander, NF
346 km Apr. 21

Port-aux-Basques, NF
882 km May 6

Sheet Harbour, NS
1,278 km May 15

Dartmouth, NS
1,373 km May 20

Charlottetown, PEI
1,728 km May 26

Saint John, NB
1,947 km May 31

Bristol, NB
2,214 km June 6

Hwy 185, PQ
2,426 km June 11

Quebec City, PQ
2,663 km June 15

Montreal, PQ
2,917 km June 24

Hawkesbury, ON
3,030 km June 28

Ottawa, ON
3,123 km June 30

Pickering, ON
3,488 km July 9

Toronto, ON
3,523 km July 11

Hamilton, ON
3,622 km July 14

London, ON
3,771 km July 17

Gravenhurst, ON
4,153 km July 28

Sudbury, ON
4,430 km Aug. 4

Sault Ste. Marie, ON
4,675 km Aug. 12

Wawa, ON
4,901 km Aug. 18

Terrace Bay, ON
5,153 km Aug. 27

Thunder Bay, ON
5,373 km Sept. 1

LABRADOR

QUEBEC

N F L D

P E I

N S

N B

ONTARIO

Hudson Bay

ATLANTIC OCEAN

Courtesy of the Terry Fox Foundation

freezing, but I wasn't wearing sweats so people could see my leg. I'd run just over twenty-eight miles."

May 29: 1,865 km   Highway 2, west of Moncton, NB
"We learned that Saint John would have nothing organized for us. I try so hard and then get let down. I am going to run right down this city's main street. Doug is going to follow behind and honk. We will be rebels, we will stir up noise. People will know Terry Fox ran out of his way to Saint John for a reason!"

June 6: 2,214 km   Bristol, NB
"The first few miles were the usual torture. My foot was blistered bad, but my stump wasn't too bad. Today I had tremendous support. Everybody honked and waved. People all over looked out of their homes and stores and cheered me on."

June 7: 2,256 km   Perth-Andover, NB
"In the town there was tremendous support and it quickened my pace up for the remaining fourteen miles. I flew!"

June 11: 2,426 km   Highway 185, PQ
"The wind howled again all day. Right in my face. It was very difficult constantly running into the wind. It zaps it right out of your body and head. The only people here who know about the Run are the truckers and the out-of-province people. Everyone else wants to stop and give me a lift."

June 13: 2,592 km   Highway 20, PQ
"I am tired and weary because people are continually forcing me

off the road. I was actually honked off once. People are passing from behind me on this narrow road. It is so frustrating."

June 15: 2,663 km   **Quebec City, PQ**
Terry is honoured by meeting Gérard Côté, four-time Boston Marathon winner, and is featured on the front page of the French-language daily *Le Soleil*.

June 23: 2,917 km   **Montreal, PQ**
Terry runs into Montreal with Montreal Alouette kicker Don Sweet and four wheelchair athletes.

June 28: 3,030 km   **Hawkesbury, ON**
Terry is welcomed to Ontario by a crowd of two hundred, a band playing and thousands of balloons, which read, "Welcome Terry. You Can Do It."

June 30: 3,113 km   **Just outside Ottawa, ON**
"Everybody seems to have given up hope of trying. I haven't. It isn't easy and it isn't supposed to be, but I'm accomplishing something. How many people give up a lot to do something good? I'm sure we would have found a cure for cancer twenty years ago if we had really tried."

July 1: 3,123 km   **Ottawa, ON**
Terry kicks the opening ball of a CFL exhibition game between Ottawa and Saskatchewan. He receives a standing ovation from a crowd of over sixteen thousand as he kicks the ball with his good leg.

July 6: 3,412 km   **Millbrook, ON**
Terry collapses in the van from exhaustion—his face brilliant
red, his breath laboured, his eyes closed as if blocking out the
light and the pain, a wrinkled $100 bill, damp from perspira-
tion, clasped tightly in his hands.

July 9: 3,488 km   **Pickering, ON**
John and Edna Neale wait hours for Terry to pass by. When they
finally see him, they say, "He was just what was needed to give
us a little pride in our own people, the same kind Americans
have in abundance."

July 10: 3,508 km   **Scarborough, ON**
Terry tells several thousand people at the Scarborough Civic
Centre that his run is not meant to make him famous, he isn't
interested in wealth or notoriety and that he is just a guy
running across the country to collect money for cancer
research. He also says that the Marathon would have to continue
even without him.

July 11: 3,523 km   **Toronto, ON**
Terry meets his hockey idol Darryl Sittler, who gives Terry his
1980 NHL all-star team sweater. Darryl says, "I've been around
athletes a long time and I've never seen any with his courage
and stamina." One onlooker comments, "He makes you believe
in the human race again."

July 14: 3,622 km   **Hamilton, ON**
Terry is mobbed by teenagers and women after he speaks at the
Royal Botanical Gardens and raises $4,500. As well, the 1960

Canadian Marathon champion, Gord Dickson, gives Terry his gold medal, saying, "The young fellow was running the greatest race of all."

July 28: 4,153 km   **Gravenhurst, ON**
Terry celebrates his twenty-second birthday along with two thousand other people at the Gravenhurst Civic Centre. One of his gifts is a new artificial limb. The community of eight thousand people raises $14,000.

August 4: 4,430 km   **Sudbury, ON**
Terry reaches his halfway point, although for the next four hundred miles the people living on the route call their own homes the halfway point. It is discovered that the odometer has a 4 percent error, and Terry has actually run an additional sixty-five miles!

August 12: 4,675 km   **Sault Ste. Marie, ON**
When a Sault Ste. Marie radio station broadcasts that a spring has snapped in Terry's artificial limb, a welder jumps in his car to make a road call. In ninety minutes, the spring is repaired and Terry is on the road again.

August 18: 4,901 km   **Wawa, ON**
The Montreal River Hill, just south of Wawa, is three kilometres long. Those who know it are making the analogy of the hill being Goliath and Terry being David. Terry's T-shirt today reads, "Montreal River Here I Come," with "I've Got You Beat" on the back!

August 27: 5,153 km   Terrace Bay, ON

Terry meets up with ten-year-old Greg Scott of Welland, who has also lost his leg to bone cancer. "Greg rode his bike behind me for about six miles and it has to be the most inspirational moment I have had! At night we had a beautiful reception in Terrace Bay. I spoke about Greg and couldn't hold back the emotion."

Sept 1: 5,373 km   Thunder Bay, ON

"People were still lining the road saying to me, 'Keep going, don't give up, you can do it, you can make it, we're all behind you.' Well, you don't hear that and have it go in one ear and out the other, for me, anyway. . . . There was a camera crew waiting at the three-quarter-mile point to film me. I don't think they even realized that they filmed my last mile. . . . People were still saying, 'You can make it all the way, Terry.' I started to think about those comments in that mile, too. Yeah, I thought, this might be my last one."

Press Conference   Thunder Bay, ON

"That's the thing about cancer. I'm not the only one. It happens all the time to people. I'm not special. This just intensifies what I did. It gives it more meaning. It'll inspire more people. . . . I just wish people would realize that anything's possible if you try. When I started this Run, I said that if we all gave one dollar, we'd have $22 million for cancer research, and I don't care, man, there's no reason that isn't possible. No reason."

Facts about Terry

July 28, 1958   Terrance Stanley Fox is born in Winnipeg, Manitoba.

March 9, 1977   Terry discovers he has a malignant tumour in his right leg; the leg is amputated six inches above the knee. The night before his amputation he reads about an amputee runner and dreams of running.

February 1979   Terry begins training for his Marathon of Hope, a cross-Canada run to raise money for cancer research and awareness. During his training, he runs over 5,000 kilometres (3,107 miles).

October 15, 1979   Terry writes to the Canadian Cancer Society to support his run: "I'm not a dreamer, and I'm not saying this will initiate any kind of definitive answer or cure to cancer, but I believe in miracles. I have to."

April 12, 1980   St. John's, Newfoundland: Terry dips his artificial leg into the Atlantic Ocean and begins his odyssey. He runs an average of forty-two kilometres a day (twenty-six miles) through six provinces.

September 1, 1980   After 143 days and 5,373 kilometres (3,339 miles), Terry stops running outside Thunder Bay, Ontario; his primary cancer had spread to his lungs. Before returning to B.C. for treatment, Terry says, "I'm gonna do my very best. I'll fight. I promise I won't give up."

September 2, 1980   Isadore Sharp, chairman and CEO of Four Seasons Hotels and Resorts, telegraphs the Fox family with

Courtesy of the Terry Fox Foundation

a commitment to organize a fundraising run that would be held every year in Terry's name. He writes, "You started it. We will not rest until your dream to find a cure for cancer is realized."

September 9, 1980   The CTV network organizes a star-studded telethon, lasting five hours and raising $10 million.

September 18, 1980   Terry Fox becomes the youngest Companion of the Order of Canada in a special ceremony in his home town of Port Coquitlam, British Columbia.

October 21, 1980   Terry Fox is awarded British Columbia's highest civilian award, the Order of the Dogwood.

November 22, 1980   The American Cancer Society presents Terry with their highest award, the Sword of Hope.

December 18, 1980   Canadian sports editors present Terry Fox with the Lou Marsh Award for outstanding athletic accomplishment.

December 23, 1980   Editors of Canadian Press member newspapers and the radio and television stations serviced by Broadcast News name Terry Fox Canadian of the Year. Terry will receive this honour again in 1981 after his death in June.

February 1, 1981   Terry's hope of raising $1 from every Canadian to fight cancer is realized. The national population reaches 24.1 million; the Terry Fox Marathon of Hope fund totals $24.17 million.

June 28, 1981   After treatment with chemotherapy and interferon, Terry Fox dies at Royal Columbian Hospital, New Westminster, British Columbia—one month short of his twenty-third birthday.

July 17, 1981   British Columbia names a 2,639-metre (8,658-foot) peak in the Rocky Mountains, Mount Terry Fox, as a lasting symbol of Terry's courage.

July 30, 1981 An eighty-three-kilometre (fifty-two-mile) section of the Trans-Canada Highway between Thunder Bay and Nipigon is renamed the Terry Fox Courage Highway in Terry's honour.

July 30, 1981 The Canadian government creates a $5-million endowment fund named the Terry Fox Humanitarian Award to provide scholarships each year in honour of Terry Fox. The award is presented to students who demonstrate the highest ideals and qualities of citizenship and humanitarian service.

August 29, 1981 Terry Fox is posthumously inducted into the Canadian Sports Hall of Fame.

September 13, 1981 The first Terry Fox Run is held at more than 760 sites in Canada and around the world. The event attracts three hundred thousand participants and raises $3.5 million.

April 13, 1982 Canada Post issues a Terry Fox stamp. Prior to this, no other stamp had been issued until ten years after the death of the honouree.

April 20, 1982 The Marathon of Hope fund now totals $27.8 million and is allocated to cancer research projects in the Terry Fox New Initiative Programs of the National Cancer Institute of Canada.

June 26, 1982 A 2.7-metre (9-foot) bronze statue of Terry Fox is unveiled at Terry Fox Lookout, a site just off the Terry Fox

Courage Highway, west of Thunder Bay, Ontario. The site overlooks Lake Superior near where Terry ended his run on September 1, 1980.

During 1983   The Canadian Coast Guard dedicates its second most powerful ship in Terry's name. The ship is recommissioned in 1994.

May 26, 1988   The Terry Fox Run becomes a trust, independent of the Canadian Cancer Society. The organization becomes known as the Terry Fox Foundation.

February 1989   The YTV network awards the first Terry Fox Award, which honours individuals or groups who, despite physical or emotional obstacles, have contributed in a meaningful way to their communities.

December 1990   The Sports Network (TSN) names Terry Fox Athlete of the Decade; the field included Wayne Gretzky and Michael Jordan.

February 11, 1994   The Terry Fox Hall of Fame is created to provide permanent recognition to Canadians who have made extraordinary personal contributions to assist or enhance the lives of people with physical disabilities.

July 1, 1998   The Terry Fox Monument is rededicated in Ottawa, Ontario, and is now part of the Path of Heroes, a government initiative to raise public awareness and appreciation of great Canadians who have helped shape the country.

August 28, 1998   The Terry Fox Foundation announces a new infusion of $36 million in funds for Canadian cancer research. The new program, called the Terry Fox New Frontiers Initiative, represents a departure from any existing research programs and will target increased innovation and risk.

June 30, 1999   Terry Fox is voted Canada's Greatest Hero in a national survey.

January 17, 2000   Terry is once again immortalized on a Canadian postage stamp. This time he is part of the prestigious Millennium Collection of influential and distinguished Canadians.